"The point is, Liv, there is nothing else. It doesn't say a time to feel sorry for yourself or give up. It doesn't say there is a time for fear or even a time to die. Because those aren't options. There is only living and fighting. That's it."

Liv sighed.

"So what time is it?" he asked.

"Time to kill," she said reluctantly.

"Try it with a little more conviction, woman." Roen laughed.

"I'll never make a good merman."

"There's a reason Salla chose you; you're strong. Stronger than she is. You just don't know it yet. And with us helping you, you'll be even stronger. Now, can I get another one? What time is it?"

"Oh, stop being so corny. I think I liked you better when you were a complete hard-ass."

"What's that? I couldn't hear you. Did you say you like my hard ass?"

Liv laughed. *"No, I said—"*

"Because I cannot blame you. It is mighty and strong like a manly oak. Or is my ass more like two halves of a boulder? I don't know."

Her laughter died down. *"I love you, Roen. Whatever happens, just know that I'm glad I got to meet you—it's been one hell of a ride."*

"The ride's not over yet, my love. It's just getting started."

But as that plane grew closer, even he could feel Salla's cold presence growing stronger. *There's no time for doubt, man. That's not on the list of options either.*

OTHER WORKS BY MIMI JEAN PAMFILOFF

FUGLY (Contemporary Romance)
IMMORTAL MATCHMAKERS, Inc.
(Book 1/Paranormal Romance/Humor)
FATE BOOK (New Adult Suspense/Humor)
FATE BOOK TWO (New Adult Suspense/Humor)
THE HAPPY PANTS CAFÉ (Prequel/Rom-Com)

THE MERMEN TRILOGY (Dark Fantasy)
Mermen (Book 1)
MerMadmen (Book 2)

THE KING TRILOGY (Dark Fantasy)
King's (Book 1)
King for a Day (Book 2)
King of Me (Book 3)

THE ACCIDENTALLY YOURS SERIES
(Paranormal Romance/Humor)
Accidentally in Love with…a God?
Accidentally Married to…a Vampire?
Sun God Seeks…Surrogate?
Accidentally…Evil? (a Novella)
Vampires Need Not…Apply?
Accidentally…Cimil? (a Novella)
Accidentally…Over? (Series Finale)

COMING SOON
MACK (Book 4, the King Series)
TOMMASO (Immortal Matchmakers Series, Book 2)
GOD OF WINE (Immortal Matchmakers Series, Bk 3)
TAILORED FOR TROUBLE (THE HAPPY PANTS
SERIES Book 1) (Romantic Comedy)

ISBN: 978-0-9962504-6-7

Cover Design: EarthlyCharms.com

Editing: Latoya C. Smith and Pauline Nolet

Interior design: WriteIntoPrint.com

MERCILESS

Book 3

The Mermen Trilogy

Mimi Jean Pamfiloff

Mimi Boutique Imprint

Like "FREE" Pirated Books?
Then Ask Yourself This Question:
WHO ARE THESE PEOPLE I'M HELPING?

What sort of person or organization would put up a website that uses stolen work (or encourages its users to share stolen work) in order to make money for themselves, either through website traffic or direct sales?

Haven't you ever wondered?

Putting up thousands of pirated books onto a website or creating those anonymous ebook file sharing sites takes time and resources. Quite a lot, actually.

So who are these people? Do you think they're decent, ethical people with good intentions? Why do they set up camp anonymously in countries where they can't easily be touched? And the money they make from advertising every time you go to their website, or through selling stolen work, **what are they using it for?**

The answer is you don't know.

They could be terrorists, organized criminals, or just greedy bastards. But one thing we DO know is that **THEY ARE CRIMINALS** who don't care about you, your family, or me and mine.

And their intentions can't be good.

And every time you illegally share or download a book, YOU ARE HELPING these people. Meanwhile, people like me, who work to support a family and children, are left wondering why anyone would condone this.

So please, please ask yourself who YOU are HELPING when you support ebook piracy and then ask yourself who you are HURTING.

And for those who legally purchased or borrowed or obtained my work from a reputable retailer (not sure, just ask me!) muchas thank yous! You rock.

MERCILESS

CHAPTER ONE

Liv Stratton stumbled through the dark cave, her eyes desperate for the comfort of daylight ahead, her blue T-shirt and khaki shorts dripping with water.

No. Fuck no. This can't be happening. She stopped and stared into her shaking hands. But she didn't see flesh, fingers, or palms. There were only two empty hands that moments ago held her very own beating heart.

Is this really happening? Is any of this real?

She pressed her pale hands above her left breast. No heartbeat.

Oh, God. She never saw this coming. And for all her degrees and smarts, her twenty-nine years of life were no match for this ancient bitch of an island. It could see five thousand moves ahead.

Liv wiped away her bitter tears. *This was the island's plan all along.* It had always been about *this.*

꩜

Three Days Earlier

"So what's it going to be, Liv? Are you or aren't you going to fuck me?" Shane, a complete cutthroat bastard with deep green eyes, shaggy jet-black hair, and the smile of a psychopath on holiday, stared from across the rustic-looking dining room table while Liv shifted in her chair. She had no clue how she'd gotten to Shane's secluded beach house of terror, but she knew he'd been planning to kidnap her for a while. His house had been meticulously gussied up in honor of her arrival—fresh paint, recently varnished floors, and new carpet in the hallway. There was even a modern-looking glass chandelier hanging above the table.

"Did you really think redecorating would make me forget everything you've done or what you really are?" she snarled over her plate of untouched…whatever-the-hell food it was. Yeah, he'd cooked her dinner. *Psycho.*

"Just the opposite." His signature sadistic smile flickered over his lips. "I want you to always remember how I killed the man you love and stole you away. Never forget, human, what I'm capable of and why you should obey me."

Oh God…Roen. Liv felt her heart cracking in two. The moment she'd woken up here, Shane proudly told her that Roen had drowned in the ocean—all Shane's doing. But her soul refused to believe he was dead. It wasn't possible.

Was it?

"You're an animal," she hissed.

"No. I am a merman." He leaned back in his chair, smugness oozing from his face. "What have *you* done for the world lately?"

Like all mermen, Shane had a superiority complex. Yes, his kind was seductively beautiful, a feast for the female eyes. And despite calling themselves "mermen," they were nothing like the creatures found in legends with tails and scales. But Shane thought himself to be some sort of god. He cared for nothing and no one. He feared nothing and no one.

Of course, Roen, the man she loved more than life itself, was a merman, too, but he had the kind of soul that instantly made a woman overlook his tough heart and menacing vibe.

He can't be dead.

Liv straightened her back. "Unlike you, Shane, I don't hurt people to get what I want. But I could make an exception." She glanced down at the butter knife next to her plate.

"Now, Liv," he warned with a restrained growl. "I asked you a question. I expect an answer." Would she or wouldn't she open her legs for him?

"Does asking for my permission to be violated make you feel better about yourself, Shane? Just wanna know. Because that's what you're doing here. You're basically asking me to choose between sleeping with you and dying."

"Liv!" he barked.

She glanced toward the window, noting how a

bit of sunlight still showed through the off-white curtains. She had to make her move before nightfall.

"Is it yes or no?" His menacing frame hunched forward in a threatening manner with elbows planted and hands tightly squeezed together, fingers laced.

Her answer was "never." *No. Wait. Make that never-fucking-ever. As in...lasting peace in the Middle East, Justin Bieber joins a monastery, and Trump shaves his head kind of never-ever.* She would *never* open her legs for him. She would never bow or grovel either. And given that this "man" believed he and she were destined to fuck, procreate, and then repeat as many times as her body would allow, well, that led to only two wonderful outcomes: *Kill him. Or die trying.* Because no one was coming to save her.

Not this time.

Thanks to Shane, everyone thought "the maids" had ended her. No, not the kind of maids who leave a mint on the pillow. These were ravenous mermaids that lived in the waters surrounding El Corazón, the island where Shane's people were from.

Liv brushed a few sticky, dark strands of hair out of her eyes. Her skin and hair were still covered with salty dried seawater from her little near-death swim.

"Shane?" Liv reached for her wineglass and began circling the tip of her finger over the lip, feigning composure. "Can I ask why you chose me?" She really didn't give a flying crap about the why; she only needed to buy time to think. She'd only been awake for a few hours and had no clue where the ever-living-merman-hell she was other than on some remote island—something Shane'd also mentioned when she'd first come to. And from the way he was dressed—jeans and a thick cream-colored sweater—she assumed they were somewhere isolated and north. Probably upper Alaska. Or Siberia? Because mermen didn't get cold easily, and unless she'd been unconscious for more than three weeks, they were still in July. Of course, to add to her confusion, he'd given her only a white tank top and some skimpy khaki shorts to wear. In any case, they could be anywhere in the world.

"Who gives a fuck? Now, enough!" Shane slammed his fist on the table. "Answer my damned question so I can get on with either fucking you or killing you."

"Yes, okay. I'll do it," she blurted out, staring into his eyes, desperately trying to hide what was happening inside her—rage, devastation, despair. *Roen can't be dead. He can't be.* "I just need a second to freshen up."

"I'm a merman. I don't care about fresh. I just care about pussy."

She wanted to spit in his face. Everything about Shane disgusted her, including his choice of words.

"I have to pee, Shane." She lifted a brow expectantly, and he answered by jerking his head to the right.

"Down the hall. First door on the right. And

don't try anything, landlover. There will be no second chances if you do."

She rose from the table, determined not to allow even one inch of this nearly seven feet of solid muscle to frighten her in any way.

As she headed for the bathroom, she again noticed the home's eerie combination of new furniture and fixtures mixed with Shane's very "special" woodworks—a two-foot-tall carved mermaid sitting on a small lopsided handmade table at the end of the hall. *Wow. That personal touch of his is about as warm and fuzzy as a cracked molar.*

Once inside the bathroom, she flipped on the lights, shut the door, and blew out a frantic breath. What the hell was she going to do?

Her eyes took in the small bathroom. It too had been spruced up with new-looking fixtures and gleaming white tile. *Please tell me he went the extra mile for my comfort and stashed a knife in here.* She paused for a moment, catching a glimpse of herself in the mirror.

Holy crap. She'd once been stuck in a life raft for ten days, dying of starvation and dehydration. Even then, she didn't look *this* bad. Her long dark hair was matted, her usually pale face looked ghost-white, and the whites of her brown eyes were red like she'd been swimming in a chlorinated pool without goggles.

I look like hell. She also looked like a woman at the end of her rope with nothing left to lose.

She yanked open the medicine cabinet. *Crap. Empty.* She then checked underneath the sink, finding only a bar of soap and a roll of toilet paper. *Dammit.* He'd "human proofed" the bathroom. Her only hope was to get back out there, grab that butter knife, and plunge it somewhere soft—his throat, his stomach, his cheek—to distract him long enough so she could get outside. From there, she didn't know what she'd do. If they were truly on another island, she'd have to find a way off it.

She looked up at the ceiling and said a silent prayer. *Whatever happens, please let my family be okay. Please let Roen be okay.*

She flushed the toilet for appearances' sake and yanked open the door, half expecting Shane to be standing there waiting with a scowl, but he wasn't.

Cautiously, she walked down the hallway, back out into the dining room. When the table came into view, Shane was not in his seat.

She swiveled on her heel, listening for him. Where had he gone?

Who cares? Run for it. She bolted through the dining room toward the living room, where she assumed she'd find a front door.

She took two steps into the next room and was tripped from behind, sending her flying into the wood-plank floor. She landed right behind the couch—an overstuffed blue thing.

"Where the fuck do you think you're going?" Shane snarled, right before he grabbed her by the hair and dragged her back to the dining room.

Liv kicked and clawed at his hands. "Fucking let me go!"

"Get your ass back to that table," he roared,

shoving her toward her chair.

She reached for the butter knife and quickly twisted around, taking a swipe at him. Shane instinctively jumped back, but the moment he realized what was in her hand, he began to laugh.

"You think you can hurt me with that?"

"It's worth a shot." She panted.

Slowly, with an amused look in his eyes, he dipped his head. "Do it, you fucking little cunt. Take a crack."

"Okay." She lunged, knocking him off his feet, but he reached out and took her down with him. She landed right on top of him with her knee wedged between his thighs. She went for it, thrusting upward. He let out a painful groan, but it didn't stop him. He rolled on top of her, rage spewing from his green eyes.

"I'll fucking kill you." He reached for her neck, and in that moment, Liv remembered the first time she'd met Shane. She'd been near death after being shipwrecked and floating on that life raft. From the moment he spotted her and pulled her raft to shore, he'd treated her like an animal. He hit her, he nearly drowned her, he punished her for disobeying because he believed she was his property. Then Roen came along and changed everything. He'd fought for control of the island just to save her and set her free. If Shane won now, it would mean that everything Roen had given up to save her life meant nothing.

"No," she growled as Shane began squeezing her neck, "I'll kill you!" She jammed the knife into his left eye.

He fell to the side, screaming in agony as blood poured from the socket.

Liv was about to run for the door when a sobering thought hit her. Mermen generally carried water from their home island that healed them almost instantly. Actually, it healed anyone instantly. Except for her. She was resistant to the water somehow—it took a whole heck of a lot of it to have any effect—and she was immune to the mermen's powers of influence over humans. But the point was, Shane was vulnerable right now. And he likely had some of that water with him. If he got even so much as a few drops, he'd be as good as new in seconds.

And then he'll kill you.

Liv swallowed down a sour lump in her throat, knowing what she had to do.

Show no mercy.

Liv quickly jumped on top of Shane and straddled his torso. With the entire weight of her body, she pushed the knife in. Shane fell limp.

"That's what I've done for the world, you asshole." Liv jumped up and away from Shane's lifeless body. "Oh, God!" *I killed him. I killed him.* She instantly hated that her life had led to this moment. She, a woman who once believed that love made the world go round, was now a killer.

Get a fucking grip, Liv. You have to get the hell out of here. Her heart began raging with the need to get to Roen. *He can't be dead. He can't be...* Shane had to be lying.

Or maybe you just don't want to believe it. An image of Roen—that silky caramel brown hair, that strong jaw, those fierce eyes—flashed in her mind. Her heart ached to see his face again. Even if it cost her life.

You can't give up hope. He has to be alive. There was only one way to know for sure, of course; she needed to return to El Corazón, the one thing she never thought she'd want. Easier said than done because it was an island that couldn't easily be found by humans.

And you are stuck on a romantic getaway with Shane's body.

CHAPTER TWO

Present Day. El Corazón Island.

This is the only option, Roen thought, gripping his hard shaft in his hand, the hot spray of the shower beating down on his back. *Not like I can* foke *a mermaid.* Even if they had the right parts, what man in his right mind would want to go there?

He let out an anguished sigh.

Goddammit, he missed Liv. The human-looking one. That…that…*disgusting thing* downstairs with yellow eyes, sharp teeth, and charcoal black skin, frantically stirring its tail in the giant fish tank, was not his Liv.

Not anymore.

Before being bitten, his Liv had soft brown hair and warm brown eyes. His Liv had beautiful breasts and sexy curves. Simply thinking of how she used to look got him hard. Case in point: the backbreaking erection he'd had since that morning, the result of a restless night filled with erotic Liv-dreams.

It was now nine in the evening.

What am I going to do? He leaned forward, pressing his forehead against the cool white tile on the wall. He was lying to himself. His heart hurt way more than his cock. Because his time was almost out, and he had no idea how to change Liv back from that beast in his fish tank—their sacred water had no effect on her.

Hell, what does it even matter now? For some unknown reason, every man on the island was dying anyway, and as much as he wanted to save them, he was too exhausted to fight anymore.

He glanced at the strange black spots covering his arms, legs, and torso, some of them now an inch in diameter. The stiff flesh in his palm deflated like a punctured tire. *Foking hell. Well, I guess that takes care of that problem.*

"Ro! What the fuck are you doing in there? Jerking off?" screamed a deep familiar voice through the locked door. It was his "little" brother, Lyle. For the record, Lyle was the largest merman on the island of El Corazón. Seven feet tall, thighs and arms like tree trunks, battle-scarred skin, and merman green eyes. Like most men here, he never cut his hair or shaved unless there was a good reason—generally having to do with blending in when they went to the mainland.

"Not anymore! What the hell do you want?" Roen called out.

"Liv escaped from the tank!" Lyle screamed.

Fantastic. She was probably looking for food. Sadly, they were all hungry, but there was no way on or off the island. For some mysterious reason, the maids—almost two thousand of them—surrounded the shores, blocking the harbor. No, he and his men couldn't kill them—those maids were like his Liv downstairs in that tank. Monsters or not, mermen felt protective of their females.

His other option, to call someone from his shipping company to bring food by plane or a boat, was a nonstarter, as well. Humans couldn't see El Corazón unless they were right on top of it, and if they managed to spot it, the island had a way of making sure unwanted visitors died before ever stepping one foot on shore. He couldn't sentence one of his employees to die.

"What do you want me to do?" Lyle screamed.

"How the hell should I know?"

"She's *your* mate!" Lyle replied.

Meaning, Lyle was not at all thrilled about going through the house looking for the thing. A maid was ten times stronger than a merman and, from what he could tell, they were only five percent human. The other ninety-five percent was pure savage animal.

But she's your Liv. God, how he loved her. Could their lives be any more of a goddamned mess? He tried reminding himself to be grateful Liv was even alive. She'd been thrown to the maids by Shane's men—a punishment for breaking some law, which was a lie.

That didn't matter now. What mattered was Liv had survived somehow. Of course, she'd been bitten and transformed—something he hadn't even known to be possible. He thought only a merman's bite changed a woman. However, on this island, anything was possible. *Usually bad possibles.*

"*Foke.* I'll be there in a minute," Roen yelled. "Tell the men to leave the house." God forbid Liv eat one of his guards.

"Hurry the *foke* up, then," Lyle barked as Roen turned off the water and stepped out, grabbing a towel from a hook on the wall. The "foke" was a jab at Roen's Scottish accent. It only came out when he swore or really lost his temper.

As Roen dried off in his luxuriously appointed bathroom of imported white Italian marble, he couldn't help thinking how ridiculous it was to be out in the middle of the Pacific, living like this and pretending to be civilized. He wasn't simply referring to the bathroom—his home, for example, was a modern, two-story palace. They also had a science center with state-of-the-art equipment for studying the island. They had solar power and a small medical clinic. There was every luxury known to the human world on this island, yet their world was the same savage nightmare it had been for the last few thousand years, centered on protecting this evil island. And for thousands of years his people had been bowing to her, obeying her, killing for her. All because they believed she was sacred. All because someone somewhere—long before his time—claimed the world could not go on without her.

He had to wonder, though, was she really the

heart of the planet? Did her water really create the spark of life in all living creatures following conception? That was what their folklore said, but he simply couldn't believe it. Something so evil couldn't possibly create life.

Doesn't matter. We're all done kneeling to her. And they might be dying from this mysterious illness now, but at least they were free.

Roen finished toweling off and then tied a long piece of soft suede around his waist to cover his lower torso. Modesty was a human concept, but the men here were unbendable when it came to tradition. Getting naked was reserved only for fighting or fucking.

He tied back his jaw-length hair with a small piece of leather and then opened the door, expecting to see Lyle. Instead, he heard screaming somewhere inside the house.

What the foke! Roen dashed through his bedroom, following the sounds of the grunts and cries downstairs.

It was his brother. *Foking hell.*

When Roen arrived to the large open living room, he froze. Lyle was on his back next to the stone fireplace, the mermaid hunched over him, her sharp teeth inches from his throat.

"No! Liv, let him go!" Roen demanded with his deep, authoritative voice, distracting her for a moment. It was enough for Lyle to tip her over and plow his large fist into her face. Liv shrieked and reeled back, but the blow hadn't injured her.

She hissed and then lunged for her Lyle-meat.

Roen rushed to block her and they collided in midair. He fell to the ground, hearing the sound of bones crunch. He looked at his shoulder and realized she'd torn a massive chunk right out of him, blood everywhere.

He yelled and tried to use his good arm to push her off, but she was too hungry and he was too weak. A small part of him wondered if this wasn't meant to be. He always said he would die for her. His Liv. The one woman in the world who'd been brave enough to love him.

Roen suddenly heard a loud grunt and the maid went limp on top of his body. Roen looked up at Lyle, who hovered over them with a bloody machete in his hand.

Where had he gotten it?

"No. No. What have you done, Lyle?" Roen felt every particle in his body crumbling under the cold weight of anguish. "What the hell have you done!"

The look in Lyle's green eyes could only be described as despair. "I am s-s-sorry," he stuttered. "But it was either you or her."

Roen rolled her body off and gazed into her yellow eyes. "Liv." He brushed the thick ropes of black, seaweed-like hair from her face. "Can you hear me?" He panted his words. "Don't go. Please don't go…" But the blood had already begun forming a sticky dark red pool around them.

The creature gazed up at Roen. "Love you," she murmured before the life vanished from her eyes.

꘎

Trying not to think about the enormous limp form on the dining room floor, Liv began searching Shane's beach house for a phone. She started in the small, immaculate kitchen with sparkling-white appliances, but found nothing except for some pantry items and new cooking and eating utensils. Shane really had been feathering his "love" nest for a while.

Sicko.

She opened the door that led to a back porch, wondering if there might be a satellite dish on the roof or a landline leading inside.

Again, she saw nothing.

There has to be something. Shane wouldn't have zero communication with the outside world. Mermen were paranoid about humans. They monitored their every move. That required at least a cell phone or Internet.

Liv went back inside and made her way to the single bedroom toward the end of the hallway right next to the bathroom. Like the rest of the house, it was clean and simple and smelled like new carpet. The moment she looked at the king-sized bed with its fresh linens, a violent wave of nausea hit her. He'd purchased the thing for their "fucking," no doubt.

Killing him had been too kind.

She made her way back through the dining room—*don't look, don't look*—and living room, to the front door. When she opened it and stepped outside, a cold gust of ocean air slammed into her. She bit back a hard shiver, but it wasn't the wind that evoked the reaction. It was the sun setting over the wide, blue ocean.

Oh, God. I really am on another island.

But she wasn't about to spend one more minute than she had to inside that house let alone an entire night. So if there were no phones to call for help, there had to be a boat.

Barefoot, she made her way down the sandy, wood-plank steps to the beach. In each direction, she saw only long stretches of shoreline.

No boats? No dock? She wanted to scream.

There had to be a way off this hellhole. She ran along the beach, hoping she might see some signs of civilization up around the bend, but when she got there, she merely found more uninhabited beach. Inland looked to be forest.

Winded, she doubled over and took a moment. That was when she noticed the blood on her hands. Her stomach knotted, and she made her way to the shallow salty waves. She cupped her shaking hands, filling them with water, and began scrubbing off the sticky blood. She needed to calm down and think rationally about all this.

Another gust of freezing, salty air slammed into her, making her wet hands sting from the cold. Her toes were already numb.

Liv glanced back at the beach house that sat on wooden stilts, its wash of faded white paint giving it more of a grayish color. She had to go back inside. She had to find warm clothes and shoes. Then she would keep looking for Shane's…

You're an idiot, Liv. Where did any man keep his

cell phone?

Oh, God. In his pocket.

Liv took a breath, allowing the frigid ocean air to fill her up like a stiff drink. "Okay. He's dead. There's nothing to be afraid of," she whispered to herself. *Except facing the fact you just killed a man with a fucking butter knife.*

But he would've killed her, no question about it. And that was what she had to keep reminding herself.

Liv walked back toward the house, the fading sunlight now casting a morbid shadow over the dwelling.

She made her way up the sandy steps, her body trembling so hard, she thought she might finally vomit. *Phone. Phone. You need that phone.* Liv entered the home and made her way into the dining room and immediately jumped back, pressing her back to the wall.

The body was gone.

No, no, no. Liv's heart nearly thumped out of her chest. Where was he? *Oh God.* She hadn't killed him, and now he was going to slaughter her. This was straight out of every horror movie she'd ever seen.

Liv's eyes then noticed a trail of blood smeared across the gleaming hardwood floor, leading into Shane's kitchen. Then she heard it. That sound she'd never forget in a million years. It reminded her of an animal trapped in hell, crying out for its soul. It was the sound of hunger and pain.

Mermaid. Liv's eyes went wide.

But this couldn't be right. *Why would a maid be here?* Had he brought some along to protect his home? *Or to keep me from leaving.*

She tiptoed toward the kitchen, listening to a crunching sound. *Oh shit. That's definitely a maid.* And it was...eating something. *Shane.*

She winced and then glanced over her shoulder, looking for something—anything—to fight the monster off of him. She needed that phone.

She went over to the table, picked up one of the chunky wooden chairs, and tiptoed over to the kitchen doorway.

One. Two...three! She rushed in and immediately spotted the inky form, at least twelve feet long, its long black tail fluttering against one of the bottom cabinets like a happy cat snacking on a tasty mouse. The back door had been left wide open. She'd let it in.

Liv swung hard, hitting the maid in the back of the head. The thing wailed and fell to the side, but the creature quickly shook it off. It popped up on its hand, lifting its muscular torso from the floor, and then zeroed its horrifying yellow eyes right on Liv's face.

Liv swung the chair again, but this time the maid caught it with its sharp, black claws.

"Mine," it growled.

Oh shit. Oh shit. Obviously, the maid wasn't talking about Shane's chair.

"I-I-I don't want him," Liv blurted out, suddenly wondering why the creature hadn't attacked. "I just want the phone in his pocket." She had no idea why she'd said that, because rationalizing with this thing was clearly moronic. But then again, she'd once gotten a maid to back off of Dana, her younger sister, by threatening it.

Keeping her eyes locked on the creature, Liv pointed to Shane. "Phone. It's in his pocket. That's all I want." At least, Liv hoped there was a phone.

The thing blinked at her, its razor-sharp teeth dripping with blood. Suddenly, it pulled away from Shane. The thing then flipped its tail out the back door, leaving half its enormous body—the dangerous half—still inside. There were only four feet at best between the maid and its meal. Was it a trap? Was the maid just waiting for Liv to get closer so she could attack and have her for dessert?

"Go all the way outside," Liv commanded, realizing how insane it was to demand anything from this creature.

The thing looked like it didn't understand, but then it slithered back several more feet, placing its head and arms just outside the door.

Okay. She listened to me. And she'd followed Liv's instructions to a tee. It was now outside.

Liv didn't want to push her luck with this game of Simon Says, so she took her chance, stepping slowly toward the body. When she glanced down, Liv almost hurled. The maid had been eating Shane's foot.

Oh, God. Don't look. Don't look. She reached for his front pockets but found them empty. It took everything she had not to cry, but she didn't. She rolled Shane over and spotted the faint outline of a rectangle in his back pocket.

Thank God. She grabbed the phone and jumped back.

The maid looked at Liv expectantly as she turned to leave, but then Liv had to wonder… She knew Shane had been mated because men on El Corazón wore only three colors of those little man-skirts. Red meant they were single. Black meant they'd been mated. Brown suede was worn only by the leader and elders. Shane had always worn black. Of course, being mated in their world had nothing to do with monogamy, but mates were bound to each other.

And they go crazy if they're separated for too long. "Are you his woman?"

The creature glanced down at the body and then back at Liv. "Not. Any. More," it said, with a voice so scratchy and deep that it reminded Liv of those poor people who spoke with voice boxes after getting throat cancer. Then the thing smiled at her. A giant, bloody smile flashing those sharp, sharp teeth.

Jesus. Liv backed out of the room. "He-he's all yours, the-then." Liv bolted outside with the device in her hand. The sunlight had almost completely faded, and if more of those creatures were around, this was the time of day they went hunting for food. On land.

Liv headed into the forest, away from the waves, and didn't stop running until her feet were completely numb.

She sank down under a giant pine tree, panting

hard, her body burning from the adrenaline and her lungs burning from the cold. She pressed the button on the phone, and her hopes sank.

Password? She laughed bitterly toward the sky. Of course, Shane would have a password on his damned cell phone.

"You fucking bastard!" He'd been such a miserable asshole that his own mate couldn't wait to feast on his body and tear him to pieces.

Liv stared at the phone in her hand, feeling like she was being taunted by the universe. It even had reception bars. Four of them. All the way out in the middle of the damned…

Wait. There wouldn't be cell service out in the middle of nowhere. And this sure as hell wasn't a satellite phone. Those were chunky with an antenna as thick as a magic marker. Roen had had one when she'd first met him on El Corazón. This was an iPhone.

Meaning, she wasn't on a secluded island?

She decided to try the Emergency button on the phone. After two rings a woman answered. "911 operator. What is your emergency?"

Liv began to bawl. Shane had slipped up for the second time that day. First, he'd underestimated her, and second, he'd forgotten to disable the emergency feature.

And now I'm saved. As that thought crossed her mind, however, she knew deep down inside that she wasn't. Because if Roen was really gone, her heart would never recover.

"Hi, my name is Liv Stratton. I need help."

CHAPTER THREE

"Brother, please drink this." Sitting on the edge of Roen's extra-large four-post bed, Lyle shoved a nearly empty glass bottle into his limp hand. "I found this hidden in the back of a cupboard."

"I don't want it," Roen grumbled. The agony of his wound had been so fierce that he'd been drifting in and out of consciousness for the last few hours, but part of him welcomed the pain. It was a distraction from his aching heart.

Liv was gone.

"Don't be a fool," Lyle grumbled, flipping on the lamp on the nightstand. "It's not much, but it will heal you and keep you alive. At least for a little while longer."

"Turn that off. I like the dark." Roen squinted at the bright light. "And I don't want to heal. I want to die. Save the water for yourself or one of the men." The sacred pools inside the Great Hall had run dry days ago. They hadn't known they were going to get sick, so what little supplies they'd had, they'd given to some of the maids to restore them back to their human state. Sadly, they'd only had enough water on hand to help sixty or so women out of roughly two thousand. Better than nothing, but not nearly good enough.

"The men? What good would this do them?" Lyle asked. "There are almost two hundred lying in their homes dying, praying that *you* will save them."

Roen didn't care. He'd given everything he had to free his people from the sadistic grip of El Corazón, but in the end, he failed. And he'd lost Liv. "Go, brother. Go enjoy your final days of life."

"Eh-hem," said a deep voice from the doorway. Roen looked over, across the large bedroom, to find two familiar faces: Holden and Jason. Holden was the island's doctor, a Harvard grad, actually. Which was shocking when one looked at his pale green eyes and long, wild, curly red hair—so red, it almost matched the color of the cloth he wore around his waist. He looked like one of those peaceful hippy sorts. Except for the large muscles. And until someone messed with him. The man could fight.

Then there was Jason, a tall blond with a bushy beard, black tribal tattoos over most of his body, and a fierce gaze. He looked like he ate kittens for breakfast but was really a foking goof-off—more than usual lately, because he'd been one of the lucky ones. His mate, Amelia, was the first to be transformed back from a maid. Which was why Jason, who'd once been loyal to Shane, pledged his life to Roen.

A lot of foking good it did him. Roen noticed how both men looked fatigued, their normally tall and sturdy bodies sagging and their skin covered in spots.

"Sir?" said Holden, the redheaded man. "I just came by to see if you need your bandages changed."

"No. Thank you." Roen winced from the pain and closed his eyes for a moment. "Bandages won't save me now. Just go home and rest."

Holden's pale green eyes blinked with concern. He didn't like that idea. "I need to care for the men."

Roen shook his head. Everyone needed to accept what he had. It was over. They lost. Death would bring the freedom he'd been unable to give them all. "What do you and the other doctors on the island believe is happening to us, Holden?" Roen knew that Holden had already spoken to the two other PhDs they had on the island—both had been working in their science center, studying the mermen and the island.

"We're growing weak, sir," Holden replied.

"And we're dying, aren't we?" Roen asked.

Holden and Jason exchanged glances.

"Answer him," Lyle prompted, still sitting on the edge of the bed.

Holden took a deep breath. "That's my best guess at this point, yes."

Roen closed his eyes for a moment. "Then I thank you for your service," he whispered. "Now go enjoy your final hours."

There was a long moment of silence. "Goodbye,

Roen. It's been an honor." Holden disappeared, but Jason simply stood there.

"What?" Roen grumbled.

"That's it? You're just giving up," Jason said.

Roen sighed. "No. I'm dying. And so are you. Go be with your mate." None of the women appeared to be sick, but why would they? They were cured and back to their human form. This illness only affected mermen, obviously.

"There has to be something we can do, Roen. I need more time with Amelia."

Roen tilted his head toward Jason, who'd stepped inside the room. The light from the lamp illuminated the pain in the man's eyes.

"I'm sorry, Jason. But unless you're prepared to ask the island for help—something I'm not so sure would work anyway because apparently she's dying, too—then we've reached the end of this journey. And now it's time for us to take the next one."

"I wish we simply had more time," Jason said.

"So do I, but stop wasting what you've got left, sitting here speaking with me. Go be with your mate."

Did he not understand how lucky he was?

"Yes, sir." Jason turned to leave and then stopped. "Oh, I almost forgot. We searched every inch of the island. The Elders are nowhere to be found."

Roen had hoped that one of them might know what was happening, but apparently they were gone. *Abandoned ship like a bunch of foking rats.*

That, or they're dead. However, at least in Naylor's case, he had to admit how odd that was. Naylor was the oldest, the most loyal to the island. He once told Roen that the island was his home; he would never leave her. *A captain who'd proudly sink with his glorious ship.* It was a sentiment held by many men who'd followed the island blindly, like cult members. They never questioned the daily rituals honoring her and giving her thanks for their sacred water. They never doubted the logic or motives of killing fellow mermen simply to please her. They never even saw the wrong in collecting human women and bringing them back to the island to serve their own selfish needs. The island had successfully brainwashed so many of them, using their inherent trait of loyalty against them.

Perhaps that was the one good thing coming out of all this: everyone finally saw the truth. The island was not a god, and in the end, they were only left with each other.

"Thank you, Jason. May you find peace," Roen mumbled, not knowing what else to say. Getting sentimental was not the way of a merman.

Jason gave a quick nod and disappeared.

Lyle immediately let out a growl, his green eyes tinged with fury. "You fucking bastard. You are not going to sit there feeling sorry for yourself and give up like this."

What does he want? A ceremony to mark the end? A speech? Because short of those two things, there was nothing left for him to do.

"It's called defeated, not giving up," Roen said.

"The island is dying, Liv is gone, and I have nothing to offer those men. No food. No water. No hope. And to make matters profusely dire, a bunch of crazy asshole humans are now searching for this place and will probably find us."

It was a long, complicated story, but somehow Liv's hometown doctor, a woman named Dr. Fuller, had gotten a hold of their sacred water. She'd sent it to a lab for analysis and discovered some rather "peculiar" healing properties that got leaked to the tabloids. The part Roen couldn't understand was how anyone had tied it back to a "mysterious island in the North Pacific." Hundreds of ships were out looking for this place, so it was only a question of time before they found it. All of them. Not even the island herself could fend off that many humans.

Shaking his head of shaggy long brown hair, Lyle stood and placed his hand on his hip. "Roen, you can't abandon the men when they need you."

But he could. And it was exactly what he intended to do. He'd already lost huge amounts of blood and those black spots covered most of his body.

"Let me die in peace, Lyle."

"For fuck's sake. Die, then, you fucking asshole." Lyle turned and hobbled from the room. He too was weakening, his skin covered in spots.

Yet another reason for me to go first. The last thing Roen wanted now was to see his little brother die. How much pain can one man bear?

Roen closed his eyes, feeling the pull of darkness and sweet, sweet unconsciousness. He prayed that this time he wouldn't come back. The pain in his heart and body was too great.

"Your brother is right, you know," said a soft female voice.

Roen now stood near a great bonfire in the middle of a forest with soaring pine trees. *I am on the island*, he realized. Only, it looked so different now. Flowers bloomed on every inch of ground—reds, yellows, blues. And the trees were green again.

He glanced over at the fire, where hundreds of luminescent forms danced. He felt so much peace.

Was he finally dead?

"You cannot give up, Roen," said that female voice again, this time from behind him. He turned and saw the shape of a woman made of pure light. Who was she?

"I want to be with Liv," he said. "Where is she?"

"She's on her way." The woman raised her arm and pushed Roen's chest.

He fell back, his body falling endlessly toward the ground that wasn't there. "Liv!" he yelled, grabbing for thin air. "Liv!"

Wrangell, Alaska

Wearing a hunting blanket around her shoulders, Liv rushed down the plane's narrow staircase and across the tarmac of the small private airport, to her parents, who waited just outside the one-room terminal building. It was four in the morning and the sun was just coming up, but she easily made out her father's drooping thin frame wrapped around her mother.

Liv ran all the way, trying not to trip in the large slip-on tennis shoes she'd been given by the rangers who'd found her first.

She reached her parents and threw her arms around them, squeezing as hard as she could. "Oh my God. I missed you guys so much." Her father broke down and began to cry. "I'm so sorry about all this," Liv sniffled.

No, it wasn't her fault, but that didn't mean she wasn't sorry. She could only imagine what they'd been through. A few months ago, Liv had been shipwrecked and presumed dead. After that episode, she'd only been home a few months when she and Dana were kidnapped—yes, by Shane—right from her parents' fortieth wedding anniversary party. She and her sister were then taken by boat to El Corazón, where Shane had planned to lay a formal claim on Liv and take over the island. Dana had simply been a pawn, meant to provide Shane leverage and make Liv obey him. Obviously, none of that worked out and she ended up with Shane in that beach house. Roen and Lyle had thankfully managed to get Dana on a plane home before things got *really* ugly.

And by really ugly, you mean Roen dying.

Liv pushed back hard on her negative thoughts. *You don't know that. You just don't.* But every ounce of sanity she had left was hanging on by a very tattered thread.

As her parents held her tight, all three of them sobbing, news cameras appeared from nowhere and surrounded them.

Fucking vultures. These people had relentlessly stalked her for over a month after her first rescue. She could only imagine how long they'd camp out in front of her parents' house this time.

Too bad for them, I'm not sticking around, she thought quickly. *Oh, God. How am I going to explain this to my parents?* Her first priority, after spending a little time with her family, was finding a way back to El Corazón. Yes, she was going to return, and this time, she probably wouldn't come home.

Ever.

That place was beyond dangerous because the fucking island was some mysterious being, psycho and sadistic all the way. Of course, the "people" who lived there believed their home was sacred, but Liv suspected the island was just a parasite that fed off the mermen's power. Whatever the truth, there would be no peace in Liv's life until she found out what happened to Roen.

Liv pulled away and looked up at her mother, who had the same long brown hair and wide brown eyes as her and her two sisters. "Where's Dana?" She would've expected to see her here.

Her mother opened her mouth, but nothing came out except a heart-wrenching gasp.

Liv immediately looked at her father, who'd removed his thick glasses to dry his eyes. His curly gray hair was ten times whiter than the last time she'd seen him.

He pinched the bridge of his nose, trying to compose himself. Meanwhile, the reporters kept taking their pictures, throwing questions at them: "Who took you, Liv?" "Did they arrest anyone?" "Where is your sister?"

Oh no. "What aren't you telling me?" Liv feared the worst.

Doing her best to ignore the flurry around them, her mother took a deep breath. "We were hoping you'd know where to look. Don't you remember anything, Liv? Anything at all?"

"What?" Liv stepped back, covering her mouth. "What do you mean?"

Roen had definitely put Dana on a plane home right before Shane's men caught Liv and threw her to the maids for dinner.

So then...where the fuck is Dana? Had she stayed on the island?

"No, no, no. This can't be happening." Liv covered her face as the cameras kept shining bright lights and taking dozens of photos. "For fuck's sake, stop it!" she screamed, pushing one photographer back. "Get the hell away from me and my family or I will fucking kill you."

"Liv!" her mother gasped, and her father pulled her away from the swarm of intruders. "Let's get you home." They dragged her into the small terminal and outside to their old gray Subaru parked in the front, shoving her into the backseat.

The reporters were relentless, screaming at her as

the car pulled out of the parking lot.

Driving away wouldn't do any good. Wrangell was a small island and the town was even smaller. There was absolutely nowhere to hide in this place.

Worried as hell, Liv drew a sobering breath, realizing she needed to stay calm if she wanted to find Dana.

Of course, this meant that going back to that hellhole, El Corazón, needed to happen yesterday. Dana had to still be there. *Please let her be alive, too. Please.* But first, Liv had to get her story straight. She couldn't tell her parents any more than she'd told the paramedics and the forest rangers who found her just a few hours south of Anchorage. Yes, Anchorage. Far enough away from civilization for Shane to keep her hidden, but close enough that he'd have access to supplies. The new carpet in the hallway should've been a dead giveaway that they weren't too remote. Not like Carpeteria made house calls by dinghy or Shane would've laid the carpet himself.

"Mom? Dad?" she said calmly from the backseat. "I'm so sorry, but I don't know where Dana is. I don't remember anything. I just…woke up on the beach outside that cabin."

"Was it the cabin where you were being held?" her mother asked.

"I don't know. I can't remember. But when I looked inside, I spotted blood all over the kitchen. Then I saw a cell phone on the counter, so I grabbed it and ran." That would not give her parents any peace of mind, but her story would be out in the news by now. And the flight attendant on the plane ride home told her that the police had already found the beach house despite Liv's attempt to misdirect them. She'd had to explain where she'd gotten the phone, but didn't want them running off and finding Shane's place containing a rather deadly and hungry mermaid. Regardless of her efforts, however, there weren't many homes in that area, so they found the house. Just like she'd said, there was blood in the kitchen. Thankfully, the maid had seen to it that there was no body.

Her father turned left down the street where they lived. The reporters were already behind them. "The police said it was some sort of animal blood. They couldn't say which kind, though."

That was because it was merman blood.

"We'll find her," Liv said quietly, trying to hide her utter panic. "I turned up. She'll turn up, too."

Dear Lord, I hope.

CHAPTER FOUR

After a few hours with her parents, where she was re-interviewed by the state police, who still had a manhunt going for Dana, Liv borrowed her mother's laptop and went into her room. She tried not to think about how she'd just lied to the world, to the very people who were trying to help, and to her own family. But what other choice was there? Send them all to El Corazón?

Sitting in her room and scrolling through news articles, Liv chewed on her thumbnail. Where was the island? How could she get there? It wasn't too far from where she'd been rescued the first time by a cargo ship that belonged to Roen. Someone had to know where that spot was, like the captain of that ship.

She would call Roen's office as soon as they opened in a few hours. No, no one there knew about her relationship with the boss, but they knew who she was. Maybe she'd tell them she was writing a book about being lost at sea.

Fiction, of course. Because her story had tailless mermen in it.

She then did a quick search for any news having to do with Roen, hoping there might be something, anything to indicate he was alive.

Nothing.

He's not dead, Liv. He's not dead and neither is Dana.

So how would she be getting back to that island? An island normal people couldn't see unless one was physically right on top of it because the place was alive and had some sort of ability to camouflage itself. And if she managed to get there, what would she do? She was no match for the men who lived there.

There was a light knock on the door.

"Yes?" Liv said.

"Honey," said her mother, "there's a call for you. It's a man named Phil. He says it's urgent and that you know him?"

Liv blinked. Phil was Roen's pit bull attorney. And a notorious asshole. *Why's* he *calling me?* The last time she and Phil had spoken—the *only* time they'd spoken—was a few months ago when he'd been looking for Roen. Phil then accused her of killing him and then proceeded to tell the press the same thing. It was a nightmare until Roen resurfaced.

Yeah, never did see an apology card for that.

Liv walked out into the living room that now looked like a crocheting workshop. Handmade throws, doilies, and pillows covered almost every surface and every piece of furniture, including the top of their old television. Obviously, her mother had recently taken up crocheting for stress relief.

"Hello?" Liv said, dragging the phone with the long cord into the den, where stacks of paper covered her parents' desk. Her father worked as an insurance broker and her mother was a bookkeeper for some of the local businesses.

"Miss Stratton, it's Phil—Mr. Doran's lawyer."

"Yes?" Her parents were just in the other room, so she spoke quietly. She had no clue what Phil wanted or knew or didn't know.

"I just saw the news that you were rescued. Do you have any news from Roen?"

Liv's heart sank. "No. I was hoping you would."

"Fucking hell. He'd better be dead, because I'm going to fucking kill him."

Nice. "When's the last time you spoke to him?" *Please say it was yesterday. Or the day before.* Or any time after she'd seen him last. He had to be alive.

Phil groaned. "Early last week. I've been trying to reach him since. It's important."

Last week. That would be before Shane had taken her, right?

Fuck. It didn't tell her anything.

Liv closed the den door so her parents wouldn't overhear. "Phil, do you know anything about his island?"

"I know everything about his island."

She sincerely doubted that; otherwise, he wouldn't still be Roen's lawyer. No person in their right mind wanted anything to do with that place. Regardless, his words ignited a spark of hope.

"You have to tell me where it is—the exact location."

"Why do you need to know?" Phil asked.

"Listen, asshole, you just called me looking for Roen. That means you don't know where he is and that you're probably worried." She lowered her voice, trying to keep herself from yelling. "And you should be. Now tell me where the fucking thing is."

"I'll tell you, but I need a favor."

A favor? From her?

"What?" she snapped.

"I'm getting close to having this island formally recognized as US property, something I promised Roen I'd do for him. But I need money. A lot of it."

She blinked. "I don't understand." With her small savings from tutoring undergrads last semester, minus her student loans, she had exactly...*Negative one hundred and ten thousand dollars.*

"You have to sign the form to release the funds," he said.

"Sorry?"

"Didn't that fucking idiot tell you?" Phil grumbled.

"No. And stop talking about him like that."

"He signed over all of his assets to you," Phil said, not sounding too thrilled about it.

Liv felt her blood pressure plummet. "Huh?"

"You own it all. His twelve homes, his cars, his ten-billion-dollar shipping company."

Holy crap. "What was he thinking? Why?"

"I thought you might know. The way it sounded: he was dying."

Oh no. Oh no. "Phil, I need to get to that island. Can you help me?"

"Roen has three company jets—I mean, *you* own three company jets. They're usually kept in Seattle. I know because I file all of the insurance and FAA paperwork."

Oh God. This is crazy. What were the odds that she would need a plane and the location of the island and that it would fall right into her lap?

A heavy knot the size of a brick formed in her stomach. The odds were zero. Which made her feel like she was playing a fixed game. That said, what did it change? Nothing. She still had to go.

Phil went on, "Call Roen's—I mean your assistant, Cherie, and tell her to send a helicopter for you. She'll take care of everything."

"Great. Okay. Do you have her number?"

Phil rambled off the number, and she jotted it down on a piece of scratch paper.

"And, Miss Stratton?" Phil said.

"Yes?"

"I'll send the information on the island to Cherie, so you'll have what you need, but the funds transfer is critical. I'll ask Cherie to arrange for you to sign the approval while you're there in Seattle. The twenty million dollars has to be deposited by tomorrow or we lose our chance."

"Twenty million dollars?" It was a huge amount of money.

"That was the price to buy a few friends in Moscow. The island is in international waters and nobody in Congress wants to stir up crap with Russia—they had to sign off."

Russia? Congress. Were they in a spy novel now? It dawned on Liv that this situation was much bigger than just finding Roen and her sister. There was a larger issue of keeping that island isolated. Roen had wanted it protected from people, but the way she saw it, people needed to be protected from Her Holy Evilness.

Then the harsh reality hit Liv. If Roen *was* dead, there would be no one else to deal with this. *But he's a public figure. He's...fucking Roen Doran.* The man was no stranger to *Forbes* covers and power meetings with world leaders. She had absolutely no idea how to run his company or influence people or make sure the island was contained. And frankly, deep down in her heart, she only cared about finding her sister and Roen. All of that other stuff was...well...*okay, it's important, too*, she conceded.

She let out a breath, realizing that whether she liked it or not, she was in charge. Roen had seen to that. It had nothing to do with money or setting her up with a cushy life. She was his mate. He believed in her and trusted her.

Which means you're just as strong as he is. It was a thought she'd never considered. But killing Shane, fighting back, was proof. She wasn't weak. She wasn't a coward. She could handle anything thrown her way.

Maybe?

Phil continued, "Miss Stratton, I don't know what's the matter with Roen, but if you find him, please let him know I did what he asked. He's like a brother to me—an asshole brother—but I promised I'd take care of this one final thing for him. Or should I say for you—you technically own everything now."

"It's a dream come true," she said dryly, realizing the irony of her holding the title to that island. "I'll be in touch, Phil. Thank you." She hung up the phone and called this woman Cherie.

As the phone rang, Liv started thinking about how a jet would land on that island if the pilot couldn't see it.

Dammit, you'll parachute from the damned plane if you have to. Not that she knew how, but she was a billionaire now. She'd damn well hire someone to show her. But either way, this was far from over, and she *was* getting to that island. She refused to believe that Roen was dead. Her heart would know if anything had happened to him. Or to Dana. Wouldn't it?

–––

Twelve Hours Later

As the small private jet approached the coordinates provided by Phil, approximately two thousand miles west of Seattle, Liv began to feel like something was watching her, expecting her. Was it paranoia or simply her nerves trying to get the best of her?

Hell no. The island definitely knows you're coming.

Which meant Liv had to be mentally prepared for anything. The honest truth was, however, she was already running on fumes and had been from the moment she'd woken up in Shane's beach house. But there'd been no time to sleep, even during this five-hour flight on, yes, the world's nicest plane.

It's like a five-star hotel suite in the sky—extra-large, beige leather seats, a workspace, kitchenette, and satellite TV.

She still found it difficult to digest Roen's two very contrasting worlds—one the epitome of wealth, power, and success. The American dream. The other savage, deadly, and, well…crap, they had monsters, mermen, and a living island. The universal nightmare. There couldn't be two more different worlds, yet Roen had managed to walk in both, be a leader in both, and be the man she loved in both. Which was precisely why she'd broken her parents' hearts and left, only leaving a note to say she was okay, but needed some time alone. It was also why she was about to risk her life to save him. She just hoped she wasn't too late. And if a hair on Dana's head had been harmed, Liv would make them all pay. How?

Hide the butter knives.

First, however, she'd had to get up to speed. Because apparently, while she'd been indisposed, a story about the discovery of "the Fountain of

Youth" had spurred a massive search for El Corazón. And she had a damned solid clue which particular human had started those rumors.

It was the ER doctor in Wrangell who'd been on call when Liv'd been punished by the island for breaking her promise not to tell anyone about its inhabitance. In Liv's defense, she'd been so messed up in the head after being shipwrecked on El Corazón and after leaving Roen behind—his choice, not hers—that she'd been going mad. She'd later learn it was because mates who were separated after finding each other went a little crazy. But the moment Liv had spoken the word "mermen" to her therapist, the island let her have it. Convulsions, burning in her veins, the inability to breathe. How did Crazy Dirt do it? Liv had no clue. But the punishment didn't stop at giving her a massive painful seizure on the therapist's office floor. Crazy Dirt went after Dana, too, landing her in the ER with respiratory failure. That was when Liv used a vial of sacred water she'd taken back from the island to heal her sister. Unfortunately, Liv left the vial behind, and it snowballed from there. Dr. Fuller found it and sent the remaining few drops to a lab. Why? She'd been suspicious when her patient miraculously healed. Later, Dr. Fuller would confront Liv and confess that she'd also had repeated dreams about a miracle water that could cure any illness. Then the tabloids somehow got wind of the lab reports, and the legend of the Fountain of Youth was born.

Now, over five hundred fishing boats and yachts

filled with treasure hunters, desperate souls, and good old-fashioned opportunists were looking for the island.

And they're all crazy people. Because only crazy people would actually believe a tabloid story and then hop on a boat in search of the mythical Fountain of Fucking Youth. From what she'd seen in the news articles online, they were close, too. A few hundred miles too close. It was only a question of time before one of them got lucky and ran right into the place. Which was why signing the bank transfer had been critical, just like Phil said. Roen had already told her his plan to hire private security to keep people away once he held the title.

Roen was a smart, smart man. *Don't hide the island, just treat it like your private, secluded getaway. Trespassers unwelcome.*

"Miss Stratton?" the female pilot—a Judy or Janna something—said over the intercom. "We see a landing strip."

What the hell? Liv rushed from the cabin into the cockpit. The pilot pointed straight ahead toward a long strip of cleared land. The sun was just now dipping into the water toward the west straight ahead, making it difficult to see clearly, but yeah, there it was: the island. Not hidden. Not spewing its odd-looking mirage of lights that made it nearly invisible.

Jesus, the island was right there. Was it welcoming her back where it intended to finish her off once and for all?

What if it knows I killed Shane?

Liv whooshed out a breath and smoothed her hands over the top of her head and down her ponytail. The Shane piece of this was something she'd not thought of. Not even once.

Doesn't matter now, Liv. You're here. She was just thankful she wasn't going to have to jump from the damned plane. Yes, Cherie, upon Liv's request, had arranged for a skydiving instructor to be on board. It was amazing what money could buy, including a two-hour private lesson by a man that had been paid not to question Liv's sanity for planning to actually jump alone her first time. But the way Liv saw it, the dire situation called for dire measures.

"Take us down," Liv said to the pilot. "But once I'm off the plane, you need to get back in the air and as far away as possible. Understand?"

The pilot gave her an odd look.

"It's not safe here for you," she clarified.

"Why?"

"Let's just say that the people who live here don't like strangers." And there was a distinct possibility that they'd kill her on sight.

CHAPTER FIVE

"Oh shit." The moment Liv stepped off the plane, she knew something was wrong. Yes, the entire island was the poster child for wrong, but this time the island looked...different. The trees were dead—brown, dried-out skeletons without leaves or needles—the ground lacked any vegetation or moisture, and the snowcapped mountain at the center was nothing but rocks. No more snow.

It looked like someone had dropped an A-bomb on the place and obliterated all signs of life.

As the plane soared overhead, she watched it fade into the sunset along with the last rays of sunlight. A hard shiver swept over her body, making her wish she'd worn something other than a blue T-shirt and cargo shorts. *A suit of armor would've been nice.* She'd never been so afraid. Because, as if the island weren't scary enough, now it screamed death, too.

It's like the world's worst resort decided to team up with hell to create a magical getaway. Even the smell in the air was wrong—a foul musk mixed with sour seawater.

She turned on her new sat phone—compliments of Cherie, who was like a damned magic genie—and then dug out the flashlight from her backpack. Liv had brought as many supplies as she could carry—tons of fresh bottled water, a small blanket, and snacks from the plane. She threw on the pack and started for Roen's house, which was a huge two-story modern mansion perched on a hill not too far from that creepy mountain at the center of the island.

She flipped on the flashlight and started walking into the desiccated forest. Suddenly, the air filled with familiar howls and cries.

Oh God. The maids. The sound put a permanent chill in her bones, but her fear of this island was far greater than anything else. It had abilities that defied reason—the power to influence people, the ability to think and produce that strange healing water. It could control the environment around it and kill people who were thousands of miles away. Roen had once tried to explain how she did her tricks, but none of that mattered. The facts were the facts: This place was alive and psychotic.

Liv's footsteps made loud crunching sounds as she made her way through what was once a dense forest of pine trees. Half had fallen to the ground as if blown over by a storm, forcing her to climb over trunks as thick as four feet or crawl under the ones that leaned together. All the while, her head and heart said the same thing: *This place is dead.*

Everything is dead.
What the hell had happened?

As crazy as it sounded, she believed the island fed off of Roen's people. It was an assumption, but given her years of studying cultural anthropology and sociology, the island's tactics—the way she manipulated and tried to keep the mermen from leaving at any cost—smelled suspiciously close to dependence. Then, during her last "visit," she'd been reading through one of the many, many books in their archives. There was a story about how Roen's people once had gifts and abilities that were strangely similar to the island's—the ability to manipulate the environment around them, for example. Liv suspected that the island was more like a parasite and needed them to survive. Not the other way around.

So was the island dying of starvation somehow? And what had happened to all of the men? She had yet to see one single merman. For the record, these were not the sorts of men you'd stumble past and not notice. Most were around seven feet tall, and they had stunning green eyes and huge, chiseled bodies. Some had their unbelievably ripped torsos covered in tattoos—fish scales, sea monsters, tridents, and other symbols—and they didn't wear a stitch except for a piece of cloth around their waists. As for hygiene, they didn't care much for that. Not that they smelled bad—to the contrary, they smelled…well, pretty enticing, actually. All part of their "charming" attributes meant to lull and seduce human women. Nevertheless, they weren't too big on cutting or brushing their hair and they swam a lot. Dreads were the standard look. It all combined into one very intimidating and noticeable package.

You could spot a merman from a mile away.

Liv arrived at the bottom of the steps that led up to Roen's modern-day palace perched on a hill. *Please, please, please let him be okay.* Flashlight shaking in her hand, Liv cautiously climbed and then approached the front door. A sliver of light came from a small crack underneath the thick, hand-carved door embossed with symbols of serpents and fish.

She carefully opened the door and noticed that everything looked just as clean and absurdly stylish as the last time she'd been here. The air, however, had a different vibe.

Despair. The house was filled with it.

Liv tiptoed through the opulent foyer—expensive crystal chandelier and brown-and-white marble flooring—and up the stairs that led to Roen's master suite.

There wasn't a sound in the home except for the wood floor creaking beneath her feet as she made her way down the long hallway lined with doors. Most led to very nice guest rooms, one of which she'd stayed in with Roen once.

She turned the corner and found Roen's double bedroom doors wide open, the space dark inside. She flipped on the lights and saw his bed—a huge extra-long king-sized thing with four posts—covered in dried blood. *Oh shit.* Her heart constricted with painful worry. The rest of the large suite—rich upholstered furniture, dark stained wood flooring and stone fireplace—looked immaculate.

No struggle. Nobody home. Nobody dead either—thank goodness. But where had they all gone?

She pushed the heels of her hands against her lids, trying to fight back her tears of frustration and worry. Perhaps they were in the Great Hall at the heart of the mountain.

Either that or in their homes. There were a few hundred cottages and cabins sprinkled around the island.

I'll start with the Great Hall. Much more preferable to running around in that Tim Burton forest at night.

She turned to leave and heard a faint groan. *What was that?* She held her breath, listening for the source, but the sound didn't repeat.

"Roen? Roen! Is that you?" She sprinted down the hallway and began pushing open the doors to the guest rooms, turning on all the lights. She found room after room empty.

"Roen!" Frantic, she ran back to his room and then heard the groan again. It was coming from the bathroom.

Fuck. Fuck. Please be him. She rushed inside and flipped on the lights. A large form lay face down in a pool of dried blood. She quickly kneeled and flipped him over.

It was Roen. "Oh my God. What happened to you?" She didn't know what to do. He had dark spots all over his face, torso, and neck. What was it?

A plague? Roen's beautiful lips were chapped and cracked, and he had blood matted in his chin-length, brown hair. The rest of his skin was pale and damp with sweat.

Liv then glanced at his shoulder, the bandages soaked with blood. *Dear Lord,* there was an entire piece of his shoulder missing. He looked like he might die any second.

"Roen. Roen, can you talk? Do you have any water?" The sacred water worked on him. It worked on all of the men from the island. One sip would heal a fatal wound.

Roen groaned. "Liv, you've come to take me."

Take him where? "No. I need to get you water. Is there any here?"

Roen didn't respond.

"Fight, Roen. Do you hear me, you bastard? Fight!"

He couldn't die. He couldn't. She stood up and started thinking. There had to be water around here somewhere. Even if it was just a drop, something to keep him from dying.

She began looking around his immaculate room. He had papers and contracts piled up on his dresser and only a few outfits and personal items in the closet—his human-world clothes.

I have to find him water.

Liv snagged a pillow and the plush burgundy blanket from Roen's bed. She returned to Roen and tried to get as much of the blanket around him and underneath him as possible. As she gently lifted his head, sliding the pillow underneath, she kissed his lips. It didn't matter what was wrong with him—mer-bola or bubonic mer-plague—she needed to feel his lips again.

"Don't you dare die on me, merman," she whispered. "You still owe me." Yes, she referred to sex. They still hadn't slept together—a very, very huge oversight on both their parts. But since the day they'd met, roughly four months ago, their life together had been chaos. Still, the moment she saw him, she'd wanted and never stopped wanting him. She knew he felt the same. So on the off chance he could hear her, the promise of hot sex could only encourage the man to hang on. Right?

Liv rushed downstairs and stopped at the front door, looking over her shoulder. She didn't want to leave him. What if he died while she was gone looking for water?

She took a deep breath. *You have no choice. You have to go find him some water.* She bolted out into the dark night, praying she wouldn't run into any hungry maids or angry mermen on her way to the Great Hall.

Roen was ready to let go now, feeling comforted by knowing that their folklore had been true. His people believed that when a merman died, he would be united in the afterlife with his mate. That had to be why Liv was there. She'd come to take him so they'd finally be together, free from pain and the island.

But why then was she telling him to fight to stay alive?

"Liv," he mumbled, "no more fighting. I'm ready…"

CHAPTER SIX

The Great Hall. Liv had never been more petrified of any place on earth. It was a giant cavern with soaring ceilings and a deadly chill in the air, where the mermen's sacred water trickled from the stone walls and collected in pools toward the back. That, in itself, wasn't all that scary. But the place had an evil, sick vibe. It was where they held violent, bloody ceremonies and many people were killed. For her, however, this would always be the place where she'd been forced to watch as Roen almost died, fighting for control of the island and for her life. By some miracle, he'd won that day and had gotten her home, but she'd never forget the moment she thought she'd lost Roen, helpless to do anything about it.

Well, now she was in a position to do something. She would not let him die even if it meant facing her biggest fears.

Liv took a breath and entered the dark, massive

cavern. The smell of mold and darkness hit her nose. She winced. "Hello?" A few wooden chairs lay toppled over on the stone floor. The throne where the leader usually sat was empty, as were a few wooden tables. Blood stained the floor in small pools.

Liv shivered.

The last time she'd been in here, there were men going mad, clawing out their eyes from pain as the island punished their disobediences. They'd finally risen up against her and she hadn't liked it one little bit.

Liv walked over to one of the gray stone walls and ran her hands along the surface. Bone dry.

"Come. On!" The clock was ticking on Roen's life. *Think. Think. Think.* Where else had she seen water?

Liv rubbed her eyes with one hand. That doctor, a redheaded man named Holden, had a supply, but she wasn't sure where his home was.

Okay. All of the men probably keep a stash. She'd have to follow the trail down the mountain and search whatever homes she found.

Liv suddenly felt a cold breath on the back of her neck. "Crap!" She swiveled on her heel, shining the flashlight around the room, but it was empty. "I know you're there, Crazy Dirt! I know you're watching me! And you're not going to win. I won't fucking let you kill Roen."

Liv waited for a response, but there was nothing except the eerie silence.

"I hope that means you're too weak to talk and

dying a horrible death." But as Liv said those words, she realized that maybe the island's condition had something to do with Roen being sick.

Oh God. I hope this doesn't mean I have to save the island. The thought of lifting a finger for her made Liv violently ill.

Don't start making up more problems. Go find water.

༄ঌ

Liv had been prepared to see dead, dying, or more sick men. She'd been prepared to see hungry maids (and run from them). She'd been prepared to go through every dwelling she could find, searching for water, and go all night if she had to. But she had not been prepared to see this.

The first cabin she'd found, not more than five minutes from the Great Hall, had a small light glowing through the front window. When she knocked, no one answered, so she burst through the front door and went straight for the kitchen. She began rummaging through the cupboards, finding them empty.

"Who the hell are you?" said a strange female voice.

"Oh shit." Liv yelped and jumped. A woman, blonde with a petite frame and a round face, stood in the doorway. She wore a white cotton dress and a giant machete as her accessory.

Oh no. There must've been another Collection.

That was when the men who lived here went to the mainland and brought back women for the world's most awesome date night, merman style, complete with deadly hand-to-hand combat to compete for the different women.

"Who are you?" the woman asked again, her gray eyes twitching with aggression.

Liv raised her palms to highlight she was unarmed. "My name is Liv. I was a prisoner on this island once just like you. I can get you out of here, but I need to find something first. The men here use this special water. It—"

"I am not a prisoner," the woman said. "And I'm well aware what their water does. It's how they cured me."

"Cured you? Of what?" Had this woman caught the same illness as Roen?

"Of being a maid."

Liv stared, wondering if she was joking. It didn't look like it. "You're serious?"

"Yes. And the man dying in the bedroom is my mate."

"I'm s-s-sorry," Liv stuttered. "Can you just…say all that over again? You were a mermaid, and—" Liv blew out a breath. "How'd they change you again?"

"They gave us the last of the sacred water, and now there isn't any left."

The utter amazement of that information was trumped by the other part of the sentence. "What do you mean 'there isn't any left'?" Liv didn't want to believe it.

The woman shook her head. "None. We've been through every inch of the island. Can you believe these idiots used it all up just to save a few of us? Why would they do that? Now, after everything we've been through, we have to sit here and watch them die."

Liv took a seat at the small kitchen table in the center of the room, feeling like the wind had been knocked out of her. All of the water was gone. All of it.

She leaned forward and scrubbed her face with her hands, groaning. *I can't give up. I can't.*

"Do you know why the men are sick?" Liv asked.

The woman shot Liv a bitter look.

"You don't know," Liv concluded.

"It started the day after I was brought back. All I know is the men thought it might be a punishment, but the island is dying, too."

Fuck. There has to be something we can do. "So how many maids were transformed?"

"Only sixty-three of us."

"Can you round them up and have them come to Roen's home? This is all connected. It has to be." She just didn't have the necessary pieces to put it all together.

"They won't leave their men. Neither will I," said the woman.

"Goddammit!" Liv slammed her fist down on the table, feeling exhausted and emotionally frazzled. Roen didn't have much time left. "Get your head out of your ass. I don't see anyone around here who is going to save them, so if you and the other ladies would like to perhaps avoid your mates dying, then tell them to meet me in Roen's fucking house. Yesterday would be nice."

The woman's eyes flickered with irritation for a moment. "I remember you now. You're the one the island said we couldn't eat."

"What?"

"I don't remember much from the time I was a maid—bits and pieces like a bad dream—being underwater, the hunger, and how my heart ached all the time, missing someone I couldn't really remember. But I remember you. I remember your voice. I remember the island telling us we had to help Shane pretend to kill you."

Okay. Weird. "Do you remember why you guys helped him?"

"Not really. I think we were told it was the only way you'd live. We didn't want you to die. But that's all I know."

Okay. Really fucking weird. "I have no clue what that means, but if you'd please round everyone up. As quickly as you can."

"What do you hope to accomplish?" the woman asked.

"We're women. We figure shit out. That's what we do."

The lady cocked a blonde brow. "I'm not sure one single landlover has the power to change anything."

Liv was about to tell her to stop talking and start moving, but then she remembered something very important. "Speaking of landlovers, have you or anyone seen a woman named Dana? She's a landlover—looks a lot like me."

"No. No other landlovers on the island that I've seen."

Dammit. Someone had to know what happened to her.

"Where is Roen's brother?" Liv asked, knowing he'd helped arrange to get Dana off the island. Perhaps he knew something.

The woman shrugged. "Not sure exactly. He stopped checking on everyone last night. But I think he's been staying in Roen's home."

Lyle had probably been the one who'd wrapped Roen's shoulder. So where'd he go? He wouldn't leave Roen dying on the bathroom floor.

Liv rubbed the back of her neck, shooing away the dread and goosebumps. There were only two rooms she hadn't checked: Roen's library and Roen's basement, where he and the elders—a bunch of crotchety, old, chauvinistic mermen—met to discuss very important mermanly things that women weren't allowed in on.

Liv suddenly wondered where the elders were. *I hope dead already.* At least that Naylor man, anyway. He looked like a mummified asshole— wrinkly with saggy skin and hazy green eyes. He was cruel, arrogant, and—okay, a typical merman. But he'd been one of the people to help Shane steal her away and tried to get Roen killed.

Liv looked up at the woman. "What's your name?"

"Amelia. At least, that's what my mate, Jason, tells me. I don't remember."

"You're Jason's woman?"

She nodded. "I am."

Jason was a tall blonde man who was one of Shane's posse. He'd thrown her to her death. "I'll try not to hold it against you." The truth was, she liked Jason in a strange way. Or she did up until the point he had carried out her execution. "And if you want to save him, get the women to Roen's. I'll meet you all there."

With flashlight in hand, Liv hit the trail, sprinting back to Roen's house. Every step she took felt like two steps back, moving her further and further away from hope. It felt like she was being tested and pushed to the edge. It had felt that way since the moment she'd woken up at Shane's.

An endurance challenge created from every fear and nightmare she'd ever had. *Yet, here you are. Still alive. Still fighting. So shut the hell up, Liv, and stop your whining. Roen needs you.*

Winded and exhausted, Liv entered the home and pushed herself up the stairs to check on Roen. He was exactly where she'd left him, of course, only now he wasn't groaning, and his skin looked like someone had taken a sponge coated with black paint and covered nearly his entire body.

"Roen? Can you hear me?" She knelt down beside him and listened to his breathing. It was shallow, barely there.

She placed her forehead against his chest. "Roen, I love you. Please hang on. I'll find a way to save you. I promise. Just don't leave me."

His chest seemed to puff up just a little higher then.

"That's right. You just keep breathing." She wanted to believe that he'd heard her. Hell, maybe he had. Which is why she said, "Roen, just know I'll give everything to save you—my life if I have to. I don't care if I die; I just want you to live." He'd given up so much to save her, and every time she thought about it, it had upset her. She never wanted to live at his expense. And though she knew he'd feel the same way about her giving up her life to save him, it didn't matter. A world without him in it just didn't make any sense.

He sighed deeply, and she adjusted the pillow underneath his head. She then removed her backpack and uncapped a bottle of water. It wasn't sacred, but at least it might hydrate him. She tried to get him to sip, but he simply lay there, out cold.

Oh God. This was so bad.

"I'll be back in a few minutes, okay?" She made her way downstairs, hoping to find Lyle. She entered the library and her feet made a squishing sound. The rug was wet and the fish tank that once held dozens of saltwater fish was now half empty. No fish. The water was all over the floor, rotting the wood and making the place smell damp and moldy.

"Lyle? Are you in here?" She walked down the long aisles of dusty old, leather-bound books. It didn't escape her that there were thousands of years of history in this archive and probably the answer to every question about this place. *If I only had time to read all of this stuff.*

"I don't fucking believe it," said a deep, deep voice.

Liv practically jumped out of her skin. "Lyle." She whooshed out a breath, taking in the view of him. His long brown hair was matted and his ratty beard looked like he hadn't combed it in months. His normally tanned face was a mask of inky splotches. Even his upper torso and legs were covered, which she could see because he only wore a piece of red cloth around his waist.

"How are you alive?" His body began leaning to one side, and he caught himself on the wall. "I killed you," he mumbled.

She rushed over to help steady him. "What's happening, Lyle? Why's everyone sick? And where the hell is Dana?"

"You're a ghost coming to take me to the afterlife, aren't you." It wasn't a question.

"Lyle." She gripped his arm. "Fucking look at me. Do I look dead to you?"

His green eyes met hers, flickering with confusion. "I put the machete in your back with my own two hands. I watched you bleed out in the living room. I fed your body to your sisters."

Okay. Eww. And gross. And… "Lyle! I'm not dead! Shane took me. He made it look like the maids ate me, but he had some sort of deal with them—or the island did—I don't know! But I'm alive and Roen is dying and Dana never made it home. So please tell me what's happening."

Lyle's knees gave out under the weight of his massive body and he slid down to the floor.

With his bare back now against the wall, Lyle's head sagged forward. Compared to Roen, who was a large, muscular and lean man, Lyle made his six-foot-six brother look like a Shrinky Dink.

"Who did I kill? Who did I kill?" he mumbled.

Liv felt terrified—what was new—but someone being dead wasn't something she could fix.

"I don't know, Lyle, but I need to save your brother and you and…" She swallowed. "And this damned island if I have to." Though she hoped to God that saving Crazy Dirt was not the answer. This island needed to die. It needed to sink to the fiery pits of hell and burn. It was evil. "Tell me anything you know." She shook him hard while his eyes fluttered toward the back of his head. "What's happening? What made you sick? And where. The hell. Is Dana?"

"Dana got on the plane," Lyle mumbled, almost incoherent.

Liv stared at his splotchy face, trying to sort through his words. "Are you sure? Are you absolutely sure?"

"Yes."

Oh crap. Dana. Her stomach twisted.

He went on, "Then Roen left. But he swam back. We broke our ties with the island and started transforming the women."

This wasn't helping her. He was too out of it.

"Okay," she said, trying to stay calm. "How did you break ties with the island?" If they'd broken ties, then that could have caused their illness.

Ugh. She didn't know.

Lyle slumped over completely and closed his eyes.

"Lyle." Liv gave him a poke just as she heard female voices coming inside the house. The women were here. And Liv had to do what any good academic might: Discard the facts that didn't fit. Include anything with a possible link. Keep an open mind.

Fuck me. She rose from the floor and rushed down the hall to meet the women, who flowed in one by one. They were of different ages and shapes, races, and sizes. Some wore oversized T-shirts and those strips of black cloth around their waists, probably clothes they'd borrowed from the men. Others wore those long black knit dresses—one size fits all—the men kept around for guests.

"Everyone," Liv said, holding up one hand, "please go to the living room."

A thin brunette with a wicked scowl growled at Liv. "Our sister's blood soils the floor."

Still standing in the hallway, Liv approached the living room just off of the foyer and peeked around the corner. She glanced at the brown spot on the wood floor. Was this where Lyle's mystery woman had died?

"I'm sorry…um…let's go to the dining room." Liv pointed to her right. That room was really more like a banquet hall with a table long enough to seat forty or fifty people. It had three fireplaces and large merman-themed oil paintings—ships in storms being gobbled up by sea creatures, mermen battling each other with swords, and a bunch of other depressing crap.

Standing, Liv waited impatiently at the head of the table while the women filed inside and gathered around the table. Seemed everyone was in a hurry to get this over with, so no one sat.

Liv sucked in a deep breath and squared her shoulders, realizing for the first time that she was about to address a group of ex-mermaids who didn't really remember much, but seemed to have maintained a little bit of that ruthless maid vibe.

"Okay," Liv said. "First, I want to say that I know it's not easy separating yourselves from your men, but mine is upstairs injured and dying, too, as we speak. So while I understand your pain, please understand what I'm about to say: Your pain doesn't fucking matter. Your broken hearts don't matter. The only thing that matters is saving the men we love. Anything else is just noise that will cease to have any importance the moment they stop breathing."

"Who the fuck do you think you are, landlover? You think you know anything about our pain and what we've lost?" growled a black woman with beautiful long spiraled curls that flowed down her back.

Liv then realized that these women had already lost their men. It was simple math. There were only about two hundred mermen, because the island kept killing them off. Roen said so. But only about half had mates—that was one hundred. She knew because she'd seen the men at one of their gatherings on her last lovely visit. Over half wore the color red, which meant they were still single, so to speak. But Roen had also told her there were over two thousand maids. Over time, the men died, and their mates, who were bitten as was the law—*thank you, evil island*—became maids. So not every woman who'd been transformed back found a happy reunion. And those who found their merman still alive now got the joy of watching him die.

This wasn't just a cluster fuck, it was an epic tragedy.

Liv dropped her head, gripping the chair in front of her. She didn't have time for consoling them or trying to make sense of this, but she needed everyone's cooperation. She needed to be strong and get everyone focused.

Liv squeezed the sides of the chair back in front of her. "I am Roen's mate. Roen is the leader of this place and is the only man I've ever met who's willing to put his life on the line for you, for me, and for your mates. He stood up to the island and sacrificed everything he was to free you."

"So? Because the way I see it, we are all here. Worse off than before." The other women nodded in agreement.

"Your mates would've died eventually. All of the mermen die serving her Holy Insanity. And if you don't believe me, look around the room. How many of your mates are still alive?"

"Sixteen," one of the women said solemnly.

Liv's heart cried out for them. "And Roen

understood that. He understood how vicious and cruelly your people have been treated. He gave everything to put an end to it."

"What the fuck do you want from us, landlover?" said the scowl-faced brunette.

Liv shrugged. "Information."

"She's fucking crazy," said one of the women. Liv didn't see who'd spoken.

Liv slipped between two chairs and moved closer to the table. "No. I love Roen. And if there's anything I know to be true in this world, it's that there's a reason for everything. Doesn't have to be a good reason, but it's there. There's a reason the men are sick. There's a reason the island is sick. All I want is to hear what you remember. Anything your men told you, anything of importance that the island has said to you. If we can understand the cause, then we might be able to help them."

The women continued glaring at Liv.

"Fine." Liv threw up her hands. "If I need to prove myself to you badasses, then pick one of you and let's step outside. Because I don't have time for this. And there's no one coming to help, no one coming to save the men. And if you think any of you frighten me after I survived Shane's little love shack, guess again."

"What happened to Shane?" a petite brunette asked.

"I killed him. Not the best moment of my life. But there was no other choice. Not if I wanted to get back to this lovely paradise and help Roen." Of course, this was a gamble sharing this information because Liv had no clue how they'd feel about a landlover killing a merman.

The women spoke amongst themselves for a moment. The gist, from what Liv could gather, was whether or not they believed her.

"Did you really kill Shane?" Amelia asked.

Liv crossed her arms over her chest. "With a butter knife."

"Nice." Amelia smiled. "I don't remember much about him, but I remember he was a prick, so I hope it hurt."

Okaaay. Well, it seemed this information won them over because they all began sharing bits and pieces about what they remembered and knew about this illness going around. Sadly, it wasn't much.

"Amelia? What about you?" Liv asked. Amelia was the first to be transformed, so she had been back the longest.

Amelia shook her head regretfully. "I don't know much. Jason told me that he got sick the moment he broke ties with the island."

That was similar to what Lyle had said. "How did he break ties?" Liv asked.

She shrugged. "He simply revoked their connection. He said they all shut her out of their hearts."

Okay, so if the island was using them somehow, feeding off of them, then she's dying because of that. But why are they dying, too?

She thought it over for a moment. *They're still connected. They're linked in some other way.* It was how species evolved when they were in closed ecosystems. On a microscale, you had bacteria that lived inside people to keep them healthy while the person provided a nice little comfy home. On a macroscale, you had the planet. Everything depended on something else for survival. On a merman-scale, this island hadn't just fed off them, it had also kept them alive because there was no other place on Earth that could've hidden them from humans for so long. Logic said that the mermen's connection to this place was more complex than simply a prisoner and captor relationship.

Liv's sat phone rang, and she dug it from her pocket. "Hello?"

"Liv, it's Phil."

"This isn't a good time. Can I call you back?"

"I'm calling to tell you I did it." His voice broke up with a bit of static.

"Did what?"

"The island is officially yours under US Law."

Owning this hunk of insanity was the last thing she wanted or cared about. "Fantastic! Gotta go now—"

"Don't hang up!" he blurted. "I'm also calling to let you know that I just checked with the Coast Guard, and they have no intention of deploying any boats to help with your little trespassing situation."

"What trespassing situation?" Her blood went ice cold.

"I guess someone hasn't been keeping up on their *National Inquirer*," he replied.

Oh no. The Fountain of Youth people. "My life is generally much too drama-mazing for that, but I assume you're talking about the crazies looking for eternal life."

"Yes. That would be them."

Excellent. This was absolutely what they needed right now: Tabloid fans looking for a free facelift. And now that the island was sick, it seemed her little camouflaging trick wasn't working.

"What about the private security Roen hired?" Liv asked.

"They need a few weeks to put everything into place, Liv. It's a big hunk of land in the middle of nowhere, and they're not allowed on it. That means getting large ships out there to patrol and—"

"Okay. I get it. We're on our own."

"That's why I'm calling to warn you, Liv. I pulled a few strings and asked my friend at the Coast Guard to check out who's near the island. Some of them are regular fishing boats, but they're looking in the wrong area. But there is another boat five miles off your shore, heading right for you. There are about a hundred p—"

Phil cut out. "Phil? Hello?" Liv glanced at the device. No reception. She remembered once Roen saying that it wouldn't work when the satellite went out of range. She'd have to call him back because she still wanted to ask if he could track Dana's plane. Jets didn't just disappear into thin air. Usually.

Liv pinched the bridge of her nose and then looked up at the women waiting impatiently. "We're going to have company—a boat full of crazy tourists or something." She sighed.

"The maids will kill them all," said Amelia flatly. Liv was unsure if the statement was a happy one or out of concern for the people. There was a rumble from the other ladies.

"They're getting weak," said the black woman.

"They're sick, too?" Liv asked.

She replied, "No. They probably sense that their mates are sick. Many of them won't leave the beach to feed. And they're very, very hungry."

Oh, dear God! What the hell was happening? Everything was converging into this giant cluster fuck of tragedy and death.

Liv groaned. "Those stupid fucking people are going to die. The maids won't be able to resist the food coming right to them. We need to do something."

The women stared at her, waiting.

"Can't any of you talk to the maids and get them to leave?" Liv asked. Didn't they speak naked carnivorous sea monster?

"It's not like that—they don't understand things the way we do," said Amelia.

Dammit.

Liv tapped her fingers on the table, thinking. What they needed was to buy more time for the men and figure out how to help them, not deal with a bunch of treasure hunters.

"Okay." Liv whooshed out a breath. "I need some volunteers—maybe ten or fifteen—to keep an eye out for anyone trying to get on the island. If we spot a boat before they come onto shore, we can warn them. Tell them there's a deadly plague on the island." Honestly, that was the best they could do right now. "As for the men, everyone please split up. We need you going to every house and doing what you can for all of the men. Keep them warm. Give them fluids if they're still awake. I'm going to make some phone calls."

The room full of women stared at Liv for a moment, and she still wasn't sure if they were going to grab her and slit her throat simply because she was a landlover who had the audacity to give them orders, or if they'd see that she was doing her best to help everyone.

Liv held her breath as an awkward vibe filled the room.

Then Amelia spoke up. "Jason told me that if it wasn't for Roen's mercy and strength, he would've been dead already and I wouldn't have ever seen him again. He said Roen was the only one who could help us. So if Liv is Roen's mate, we all know she's just as strong as he is. Even if she's just a landlover."

Nice. You're awesome…even for an icky, stupid human. But Liv would take what she could get. This was no time for ego-fests.

The women exchanged glances, and then one raised her hand. "I'll take patrol." Then another and another. They then started organizing into groups to care for the men.

Liv would've smiled or felt relieved, but she'd only managed to produce a Band-Aid. Right now, they needed a cure.

Liv hoped her next call would give them some hope.

CHAPTER SEVEN

Liv spent the next ten minutes trying to get a hold of Phil to ask about Dana's plane, but by the time the satellite was overhead again and the call went through, Phil wasn't answering his phone. It was a little after midnight in Chicago, so maybe he was asleep.

Lazy bastard. They were in the middle of an all-out disaster.

She prayed that the person she called next would answer.

Listening to her phone ring, Liv paced back and forth across the length of the long dining room inside Roen's house. The chill in the air had her wishing one of the three large stone fireplaces was lit.

Yeah. Pretty sure a toasty fire ain't gonna help you, honey.

"Hello?" said a woman's voice.

"Dr. Fuller, this is Liv Stratton. We need to talk."

"How did you get this number?"

"You were my doctor once, remember?" Liv said, with a sharp bite to her voice. "Don't tell me you forgot about the excellent care you gave me."

"So nice to hear from you," Dr. Fuller said, lacking any sincerity. "I was thrilled by the news that you were rescued."

"Yeah, well, I almost died because of you," Liv said.

"Me? What did I do?"

"You told the world about the water and then *they* thought I was the one who'd broken their laws." Talking about this place or its inhabitants to anyone was a major no-no. Of course, right now, Liv was about to really, *really* break their laws. *Don't care.*

"*They* who, Liv? Tell me." She didn't sound concerned as much as she did excited.

"I'll tell you everything. But first, explain what you learned from having that water analyzed."

"Why would I do that? The world thinks I'm insane. That lawyer of yours had my practice shut down and I had my house taken away. My medical license has been suspended because they think I'm some crazy black woman, speaking voodoo and witch-doctor bullcrap. You've ruined my fucking life."

Phil. That Phil. He really was an asshole. "He's not my lawyer—well, he wasn't. Now he is. But I can fix all that with one phone call." She wasn't sure how, but Phil could at least give the woman money or something to get her back on her feet. "The water. Tell me what was in it," Liv said.

"That's the thing. The lab didn't know. There's some compound or chemistry in it that gives it a charge. Like millions of tiny microscopic batteries working at the cellular level. There's nothing like it on Earth and there's no explanation regarding how it works. It just…works."

"It sounds like some kind of radiation." Great, now she was reciting lines from some weird version of Spider-Man.

"Nothing like radiation. More like…when the compound in the water interacts with other molecules, it fires off millions of tiny sparks."

Oh shit. Liv felt the room start to spin. That was what Roen had called the island—the spark of life. His people believed Crazy Dirt's water was some sort of catalyst that got the heart to start pumping in the very early stages of life. Honestly, Liv thought it was all just a lie, that the island was evil and using her fictitious importance as a means to justify her cruel behavior toward her people.

Maybe you're both right.

Dr. Fuller continued, "It also turns dying cells into stem cells. It's a miracle drug, Liv, and I know it came from that island. Where is it?"

"How did you even know about the island?"

"How do you think?" Dr. Fuller asked.

Liv sighed, feeling like that giant rat in that giant maze again. Every turn she made, every obstacle she encountered wasn't by chance. "Let me guess; you dreamed about it."

Dr. Fuller didn't respond, but she didn't have to.

"I'll ask Phil to look into your medical license

and I'll bring you here to the island so you can see if for yourself, but you're coming here to work. The men on the island are sick," Liv said.

"So it is real?" Dr. Fuller said triumphantly. "The island is real."

"Yes. But the water is gone and the island is dying. And I need someone who can help me figure out why."

"What are the symptoms?"

Liv quickly went through the list. "Can you help?"

"I doubt I could get there in time to do anything," Dr. Fuller replied.

"I have a plane in Seattle. Where are you?"

"I'm in Seattle now. At my sister's place."

What a coincidence. That nagging feeling throbbed away in the pit of Liv's stomach. Everything felt all so…predetermined.

"I'll have Cherie, my assistant"—it was so strange to say that—"call you shortly and tell you where to go. What supplies are you going to need?"

Dr. Fuller wasn't sure, so she merely rattled off a list of generic stuff like IVs, penicillin, etc.

"Okay. We'll have that stuff on the plane," Liv said. "And I'm sure I do not have to spell out that you are not to tell anyone about this, Dr. Fuller. Not a soul. I'm letting you come here so you can help us and have some of your questions answered. But if you take one misstep, speak one more word about any of this to anyone, there will be no end to the havoc Phil will wreak on your life." *Finally. A purpose for someone like Phil.* "Are we clear?"

"I understand."

"See you soon, Dr. Fuller." Liv ended the call, now genuinely beginning to believe that none of this was a coincidence. It was all too weird. All too manufactured, like the island was moving the chess pieces around the board and had been from the moment that fishing boat sank. She'd drifted to this place only to meet Roen, who also had just "coincidentally" been there, too. Her and Roen's powerful connection was no accident either. She was his mate. And the island had made sure they were put into a situation that would, without question, bond them immediately as well as put Roen into position to run the island. Then, the island made sure the two of them were separated—but only long enough to make them suffer, to make them realize that there was something stronger between them worth fighting for. And fight they had. Roen had to fight to save her. She'd had to fight Shane, and now she was fighting to save Roen.

But what was the point to all this? She was being backed into a corner so tight, she had no choice but to act out of desperation.

And everything is about to come to a head. She felt it.

Liv groaned with frustration. She had to go back to the Great Hall and try to confront the island. It had to know something. It just had to. The question was, what would the island want in exchange from Liv?

But first she needed to call Cherie and see what she could dig up on Dana's plane. She'd also get her "genie" working on the supplies and having the plane readied for Dr. Fuller.

Maybe I'll have her raid the local grocery stores, too. There was no food anywhere on this damned island. *Hmmm…I wonder if mermaids will eat Dog Chow? They could get a lot of that stuff on a plane, right?* She tried to imagine feeding them in little bowls like pets.

Never mind. I'll have her load up the plane with frozen steaks.

જેન્ડ

Liv had gotten two of the women to help move Roen onto the mattress she'd placed on the floor in his room. There he'd at least be comfortable and off the cold tile.

Then she tried to get him to drink water again, but he was out. So she rewrapped his wound and then covered him with a blanket.

It was impossible to look at this man—once so beautiful and strong and unbreakable—and not want to scream at the top of her lungs.

She lay down next to him, pressing her nose to his cheek. The discoloration of his skin had grown, and his breaths were tiny puffs of almost nothing. "Roen, I know you can hear me. At least, I think you can. I'm still here. I'm still trying. Just don't go, okay?"

Roen groaned. "Liv. Liv, why did he kill you?"

She popped up, shocked as hell. "Roen! I'm not dead, Roen. I'm right here."

∽❧

In the back of Roen's mind he heard the beautiful sound of Liv's voice, but the words were all jumbled up, floating around inside him. Then he was back at that fire, being pushed away by that woman who refused to let him get any closer to the warmth of the flames.

Liv is dead, he thought with a heavy heart. *I want to be with her.* "Liv. Liv, why did he kill you?"

"Roen! I'm not dead, Roen. I'm right here. Roen!"

He opened one blurry eye and saw Liv leaning over him, her face stained with tears.

Was he dreaming? It didn't feel like one. He was in his room, the smell of Liv's delicious scent filling his nostrils.

"You're alive?" He choked out his words. His entire body burned and ached.

"Yes. Ohmygod." She pressed her sweet lips to his.

"But I watched Lyle kill you when you escaped the tank," he whispered.

"No, honey." She placed her warm loving hands on his cheeks. "Shane took me from the island. I was never in any tank."

Foking hell. Who did Lyle kill? "What's happening to me?"

"Roen, the island is dying. You're dying. Tell me what to do…" The turmoil in her eyes was almost too painful to look at.

Everything around him turned to black.

৵৽৽

Liv could not bear to watch any longer. Roen had passed out, and the color of his skin was darkening even further, as if something was sucking the life right out of him.

"Roen?" She gave him a gentle shake. He was dead to the world again, his breathing now shallow pants, like his body was giving one last fight.

She was out of time.

Liv grabbed her backpack and flashlight and rushed from his room, downstairs and out the front door, sprinting toward the mountain. It was about a quarter mile through fallen trees and branches in the darkness.

The entire way there was that feeling again of someone watching her. *You're not dead, are you, Crazy Dirt? You've just been waiting for me to show up, begging for his life.* And now the island was going to get what it wanted.

"Okay!" Liv bolted inside the cavern, pivoting on her heel. "I'm here, Crazy Dirt. Tell me how to save Roen!"

Silence.

"For fuck's sake, I know you're there. I can feel your creepy fucking vibe all around me. What do you want? I'll do anything. Anything." Liv wiped the tears from her eyes, panting like mad. "Please."

"Hello, human. I've been waiting for you…"

CHAPTER EIGHT

The island's words confirmed Liv's fears. They were all nothing but giant rats in a giant maze. Crazy Dirt had been, in fact, waiting patiently for this moment. Liv could hear the sadistic delight in Crazy Dirt's voice.

"Let's get it over with. What do you want?" Liv snarled.

"It's not about what I want—it's about what you want. Water, yes?" she said with a sugary-sweet, evil tone. She knew she'd won and was savoring the moment. But what did she win? *"I fear, however, I've been weakened. And since the mermen don't give to me willingly, then I must take what I need."*

The voice was coming from somewhere inside the cavern, but Liv couldn't determine the direction.

"Roen is dying, so there's no time for your cryptic bullshit. What do you want?"

"For you and I to have a talk." The floor crumbled beneath her, and Liv screamed, clawing at

the air as she fell, landing with a splash in a bright green glowing pool.

Liv's head broke through the surface for a breath and then she saw them. Male bodies. Floating in the water. She screamed at the top of her lungs.

"Now, now, Liv. A girl's gotta eat," the voice said coyly.

Liv swam as fast as she could and pulled herself up onto a narrow stone ledge that hugged the dripping walls. Her skin buzzed and tingled, but her stomach was a nauseous knot. Five men floated in that glowing green water, one of them face up. It was that old shriveled bastard Naylor, the elder who'd ordered her to be executed.

"What the fuck?" Liv pressed her back against the wet wall. *Well, now I know what happened to the five elders.*

"Don't be so weak, human."

"What did you do to them?" Liv asked.

"They sacrificed themselves to keep me alive a little longer."

She doubted they'd done it voluntarily, although who knew? "So...what? You sucked the life right out of them?"

"Something like that."

Oh, God. She's going to kill me, too. Liv turned her head, looking around the cave. There was a small opening in the wall across the water. She guessed it led outside. She also guessed she would have to get back into that water to get out of there because the ledge she stood on didn't go all the way around. Then she heard a weird grinding sound above. Liv looked up and watched the floor of the Great Hall—which was the ceiling of the small cave she stood in—slowly close itself. Rock by rock.

"This isn't happening," Liv whispered to herself.

"But it is, Liv. It is happening."

Liv moved her gaze around the small cave, the green light of the water bouncing and sparkling off the dark gray walls. "Where are you?"

"I do not have a body."

"Then how can I be hearing you?"

"Because I'm powerful, and reaching inside you is child's play for someone as magnificent as me."

Magnificent. That didn't seem like the right word. Dangerous. Mysterious. Impossible. Sadistic. Manipulative. Parasitic. Those were all words Liv would use.

Liv looked at the small opening on the other side and then again at the water. The good news was that there was water on this island to save Roen. The bad news was there were dead mermen floating in it and the island probably wouldn't let her take any. Not without paying.

"What's your price?" Liv asked.

"Ha. Straight to the point, I see."

"Yes."

"Liv, it is no mistake I brought you here to me. I've been searching for someone like you for a very, very long time."

And I've been desperately trying to avoid you. "Searching for me for what?" Liv asked.

"Liv, I sensed you the moment your life started. I felt your soul, your energy. You are the one."

Someone had been watching *The Matrix*. "Tell me what the fuck you want, Crazy Dirt."

"Out of all of the women I've brought here, you are the first to show promise. You are resilient and strong."

"Wow. I'm thrilled with all of the compliments. Get to the point." She feared the worst.

"I will let you leave here. I will let you take whatever water you can carry to heal the men. I will cease draining the life from them. In exchange, I want you. Your body."

Liv gasped. "My body? You want to—" she swallowed the lump in her throat "—to use me like you used them?"

"Yes. Isn't Roen worth your life? Isn't the livelihood of mankind worth your life?"

"I don't believe you are that spark Roen talked about. I think you're nothing but a parasite."

"Believe what you like; however, Roen has but moments to live, as do the other men. Make your choice, Liv."

Liv let out a breath. The island was a master chess player. And she had her back tightly against the wall.

"Fine. I will give up my life for Roen's."

"You cannot tell him, human. You cannot tell anyone about our deal."

Liv wouldn't dare. Because Roen wouldn't allow her to die for him. It went against his nature—a man who protected what he loved, loyal to a fault. Hell, he'd even give his life to save the men on this island. Many didn't deserve saving.

"That's not a problem," Liv replied.

"Good. Then you are free to go."

Liv stared at the water, trying not to vomit. "What about the bodies?"

The island laughed. *"They don't bite."*

Liv looked up at the ceiling, praying for strength. She then whipped off her backpack, which was now soaking wet, and got out two small water bottles. She poured out the fresh water, cringing and dry heaving as she filled them up with sacred water.

"How much time do I have?" Liv asked.

"Days, hours, minutes. I haven't decided, human."

Liv only wished there was a way to kill this thing off. Who was to say that it would keep its word and not hurt Roen again in the future?

"Now, you'd better hurry. I do believe your lovely merman has stopped breathing." She chuckled.

No. No. Liv jumped into the water, the tears streaming down her face. She pushed past the bobbing, waterlogged bodies and climbed up to the other ledge. She gave one last look behind her. This creature was after something more, but what?

Liv ducked into the small tunnel, trying not to scream as she felt her way through. The floor was wet and mushy like mud mixed with something spongy. The ceiling's jagged edges scraped her backpack as she passed. Where would this lead to?

A faint light up ahead gave her hope. But it was still the middle of the night. She pushed on, and when her head popped out, she knew exactly where she was: Roen's basement. The room where he and the elders had met. Did Roen know this small tunnel existed?

She got to her feet and rushed up the stairs that led to the kitchen, then through the dining room and upstairs to Roen's room.

"I'm here, Roen! I'm here." She threw off her pack, grabbed the water, and quickly lifted his head. He wasn't breathing. "No. Don't go, Roen. Don't go." She poured a small sip into his mouth, hoping some would slide down. "Drink, Roen. Drink." She poured a little more and then stroked his cheeks, placing his head in her lap.

Nothing happened.

"We had a deal, you bitch. We had a fucking deal." Liv held back a sob. What would she do without Roen? She remembered telling him once that they were meant to be together because she wasn't afraid to love him. She wasn't intimidated by his stunning good looks, his defiant personality, his seemingly cold exterior. She'd seen right through him.

But now I am afraid, Roen. I'm afraid what will happen if I lose you. She felt so much anger and rage surging inside her. She could feel herself drifting further and further away from who she was supposed to be.

She hunched over and pressed her cheek to his. "I can't, Roen. I can't if you're not here."

Roen suddenly gasped in her arms, his green and hazel eyes wide open in shock. "Liv?"

"Roen…" She pushed her lips to his forehead,

clinging to him for dear life. "Thank God."

"What's happening?" he groaned, completely out of it.

"The island, Roen. The island happened." *And I have to find a way to end her hold over you. This has to stop.* For the first time, Liv understood why Roen would give anything to free his people from this place. Living here was like living on a ship sailing straight to hell. *And that crazy bitch is the captain.*

CHAPTER NINE

While Roen rested in his room, healing slowly from his wounds, Liv went downstairs to the library and took care of poor Lyle. She gave him a little water and then left him lying there flat on his back, snoozing like a log, but he'd probably be up and about in minutes. Liv then dashed into the enormous chef's kitchen, just off the dining room, and started dividing up the water into empty jars and bottles she scavenged from the cupboards. She'd wanted to give Roen every drop she had, to heal him faster, but she had to think about everyone. Roen would want that.

Liv then packed up the water and went to find Amelia.

"How did you get this?" Amelia asked, standing in the doorway of Jason's cottage, blinking at the bottle in her hand.

"Doesn't matter," Liv replied. "Please, just be sure you give it to as many men as you can." She simply would have to trust that these women would act honorably and fairly. But just in case… "If I find out anyone gave more to any one man than Roen got, I'll kill them. You hear me?" It sounded harsh. Yes, it did. But she'd just agreed to give up her life for that water, and the man she loved only got enough to keep him from dying.

Amelia nodded. "I'll see to it."

"Thanks." Liv turned to leave.

"Thank you, Liv. I can only imagine what you had to do to get this. I know the men will appreciate it."

All she'd really done was manage to buy more time. If the plane got here soon, that would buy them a little more. However, after another day or so, they'd all be right back in the same boat. Liv suspected the island was merely waiting for the opportune moment to make her grand scheme known. What would she demand this time?

World domination and an endless supply of wrinkly old assholes for her pond? She mentally cringed as an extremely distasteful and very literal image popped inside her head. *I will never eat Fruit Loops again.*

Liv gave Amelia a solemn nod. "Let's all just focus on getting through this." Liv hiked back to Roen's and up to his room. There wasn't much left to do now. Just wait. Wait and spend what little time she had left with Roen.

She walked through the doorway of his bedroom and made a sharp, appreciative exhale. His mattress was still on the floor, but he no longer looked like a man on his deathbed. His olive skin had returned. His lips were pink and plump. He looked more beautiful than ever, including those big strong arms lying over the blanket tucked tightly around his body.

"Are you going to stand there staring or come over here and kiss me?" he said, in a deep groggy voice.

Liv blinked at him and smiled, the joy in her heart too overwhelming for words. She felt like running and throwing herself over him and doing very, very naughty things—things they'd yet to do. But he was in no condition for that. Still, she wanted him so badly it hurt.

"Stand here and stare."

He cracked open one gorgeous hazel-and-green eye. "Then I'll have to get up for my kiss." He started peeling away the blanket.

"Don't you dare move." She walked over and kneeled beside him, touching his forehead, careful not to show her true emotions on her sleeve. "How do you feel?"

"Alive. Alive and grateful to see you here with me." He smiled, and it was the most gorgeous smile she'd ever seen him make, despite his heart-stopping dimples being masked by a short brown beard.

She reached for his bandage and lifted up one edge. The skin underneath was bright pink, but the missing chunk of his shoulder was growing in. More importantly, the bleeding had stopped. "It's almost healed. Do you have any idea why you're all sick?"

He shook his head. "At first I wondered if we were all going to turn into some sort of monster, but now it's fairly obvious we were all dying. I wonder if…" He winced as he moved a little on the bed. "I wonder if the water is a lifetime commitment."

No. Fuck no. "You think *that's* why you're all sick?"

"I don't know. But if it heals us and keeps us alive longer, would it be so strange that there's a reverse effect once we cease to take it?"

Liv hung her head. So they were addicted in a sense. And if the island fed off of them— their…energy…or life force…or whatever corny New Age word she was supposed to call it, then there was no way to break this cycle.

Great. It's like email spam. No matter what they did, the crap just kept on coming.

That led her back to her biggest question yet: what did the island really want? If she was weakening and starving, then why wasn't Crazy Dirt forcing her hand and simply demanding the men give her what she wanted: their allegiance and for them to let her back in. Or re-bond or whatever-the-mer-hell they called it.

Liv started pulling her hand away, and he caught it. "Where did you get the water, Liv?" he said, sounding very displeased.

She looked away. "I think you know the answer to that."

"Then let me ask another way: What did you

trade for it?"

"Nothing," she lied—yes, right to his face. What else could she tell him? That she'd be dead soon, like the elders in that pool? "The island is probably going to be overrun by crazy treasure hunters soon. I guess she found the strength to make some water for you."

"You're lying. I can see it in your eyes," Roen growled.

"Roen, you have to trust me; I'm doing what I have to."

He gave her a look, slipped his hand behind her neck and pulled her to his mouth. His lips were warm and soft, but his short beard was rough and deliciously masculine.

She sighed with ecstasy. There was so much emotion in his kiss that it went straight to her heart and made it swell.

She quickly pulled away from him before she completely lost all control of her emotions. She was just so damned grateful to see him again— breathing, smiling, alive.

"Roen, how did you survive? Shane said you'd drowned at sea." She'd assumed it happened during this thing they called the "Great Swim" a two-thousand-mile race in the ocean. The winner would get control of the island. The loser would be executed if they'd not died already. But Shane never completed the race because he'd decided to take Liv on "vacay" and expected Roen to die—the man was not a great swimmer. So ironic, given he was a merman.

"I nearly drowned, but a maid came to my rescue. She told me how to break the connection with the island, and when I figured out that I could help the men with this information, I turned around. She carried me most of the way and then got injured fighting off a shark to protect me."

Wow. "She didn't try to eat you?" Not only did the maids devour almost anything, but Roen looked especially delicious. Even now, her body felt all hot and tingly for him. Those thick muscular arms. The way his strong neck sloped down into broad, powerful shoulders. *If I were a maid, I'd totally want to gobble him up.*

"No," he replied. "And when I was told you'd been thrown to the maids, I assumed she was you. That you'd been bitten by one of them or by one of the men and transformed somehow."

So strange. "What happened to her?"

"We had you—I mean her—in the tank downstairs after she'd been injured by that shark. But she escaped and attacked me—took a huge bite out of my shoulder—and Lyle killed her."

"That's why you thought I was dead." Lyle had said she was a ghost.

"Then who was she?" Liv asked.

"I don't know, but she said she loved me. Those were her final words."

Liv covered her mouth. Unless Roen had another mate on the side, that only left one other woman in the world that would protect him and say she loved him.

"Was she your mother?" Liv asked.

"I watched my mother die in the hospital. At least, that's what I remember. I remember them putting her casket in the ground, too."

So many things in this world of theirs wasn't what it seemed. That included the fact that Roen had also believed his brother had died. Turned out, he was here on this island all along.

"But if it was her," Roen said, his voice filled with deep regret, "Lyle saved my life. She was too hungry to control herself. He had no choice but to do what he did. Even though I know he won't see it that way."

She covered Roen's hand with hers. "I'm so sorry, Roen."

"Not as sorry as I am for believing that the island would really let you leave." He looked at her expectantly. She knew what he wanted, but she didn't want to talk about it.

"I'm here with you now. That's all that matters."

"No. It's not, Liv. Where is he?" Roen growled.

Liv looked away. She didn't want to relive the moment.

"Did Shane...touch you?" he asked.

She shook her head solemnly. "No."

He sighed with relief then turned his attention down a predictable merman path: revenge. "Where the fuck is he, Liv?"

"Please, can't we talk about this later? You have no idea what I've been through and how much I need to be with you—nothing else."

He took a deep breath, frowning.

Stubborn merman.

"He's not a threat anymore. And I'll tell you everything, but right now, I just…" Her words faded, and she pinched the bridge of her nose, fighting back the tears. Their hours were numbered yet again, and she didn't want to waste them crying or feeling sorry for herself. She didn't want to think about how she'd traded her life for one more day with Roen.

Of course, I would sell my fucking soul for just one last kiss from this man.

"It's all right, Liv. We'll find a way through this." He pulled her to him and held her, stroking the back of her head with his good arm.

"I love you, Roen." She kissed his lips and lay down with him, pressing her ear to his chest. The sound of his heart was so strong now, like music to her ears.

Exhausted, and going into her third day without sleep, she drifted off.

෴

A few hours later, Liv awoke with a gasp from a horrible nightmare. She'd been standing on a cliff overlooking the ocean. The mermen stood behind her as if waiting for something to happen, their eyes vacant of emotion. *What are they looking at?*

Liv followed their gazes and spotted a life raft with a man and a woman aboard. Liv squinted, trying to see their faces. It was Roen and…herself. Then she watched in terror as the raft sank and they were torn apart by sharks in the water, the entire ocean turning blood red.

But when Liv snapped awake, she found immediate comfort. Roen purred like a kitten sleeping at her side.

She leaned over and kissed his soft lips. "God, I love you, Roen."

He stopped purring and then smiled with his eyes shut. "You woke me from the best dream I've ever had."

"Really? Was I in it?"

He opened his eyes. "Yes. And you were naked, doing very indecent things to my cock."

That sounded like just the thing to erase the terrifying images of the dream she'd just had.

She glanced down at his groin, noticing a little extra bulkiness beneath the covers. "Well, I could make your dreams a reality." She peeled down the blanket, exposing his bare muscled chest. God, he was so beautiful. Like a god.

When she completely removed the covers, she reached for that strip of suede around his waist.

He gripped her hand. "Liv, what are you doing?"

She smiled at him. "A deal is a deal, Roen." The last time they'd been together, they'd agreed they were going to have sex.

"But what if—"

"Fuck what if." She yanked her hand away and stripped him naked and then stood. She pulled off her dirty T-shirt and unhooked her bra, allowing him to drink her in. She didn't want to rush because this moment needed to last forever, but her body told her to hurry the hell up. She could feel the seconds passing, and she wanted to spend as many of them as she could with this beautiful man inside her.

She slid down her shorts and panties and then stood over him. His long, thick cock stood straight up, waiting for her.

She grinned and raised a brow. "You really are feeling better."

"I'm a merman. And you're a beautiful woman. Whom I happen to love. I could be taking my last breath and I'd still get hard for you."

She laughed and swooned all at the same time as she sank to her knees and gripped him in her hand, unable to believe they were finally together.

"Roen, I love you. Don't ever forget that." She positioned his pulsing shaft at her entrance and then looked down at his beautiful face. The only thing she wanted was to stare into the depths of those hazel and green eyes as she felt him slide deep inside.

"Liv! Are you in there?" screamed a woman. A pounding on the door jolted her from the euphoric bliss.

Fucking hell, Amelia. Just one more minute. "Yes?" She swallowed her dread.

"The plane is here," Amelia yelled.

"What plane?" Roen whispered.

"Food and other supplies," Liv groaned. *And a doctor. And maid-chow.* She still hadn't told him about the approaching boat.

Roen threw back his head. "This isn't happening."

Oh, but it was. And she couldn't justify going at it with Roen when that plane had medical supplies and Dr. Fuller on board. Liv needed to talk to her.

"I'll be right there," Liv replied to Amelia and then looked at Roen. "I'll be right back. You rest."

He blinked at her. "Like foke I will, woman. I'm not leaving your side. Never again."

His words melted her heart. "I'll be fine, I promise. I'm just going to help the women unload the supplies."

"I said no." He reached for his suede wrap, nearly falling on his face.

"Roen, you're still weak. Stay. Here. I'll be back in thirty minutes. With food." She gave him a "don't fuck with me" look. "Trust me. You're going to need your strength. Yes, I'm talking about for sex." She dressed quickly as she spoke. "Oh, and by the way, Phil said there is a boat full of fortune hunters or tourists or something who are close. They'll probably find this place the moment daylight hits—the island isn't camouflaged anymore. Any suggestions on how to keep them away?" It was about five in the morning, so they only had a few minutes left until sunrise.

Roen looked at her. "Not sure. I'll have to think about it. When did you talk to Phil?"

"I don't know—yesterday sometime—and by the way? You're taking back your company. I don't want your money or your empire. And what were you thinking signing over your assets to a mermaid?" Because in Roen's mind, she was that maid in the tank when he'd done this.

"I thought you had a better chance of surviving than me. I still do." He paused for a moment, thinking. "So what else did Phil say?"

"He asked me to sign a very big check to influence the Russians."

His interest seemed to pique. "Phil did it, then?"

"That's what it sounded like. Yet another reason for you to take back your stuff—this is the last place on earth I want to own." What she really wanted to add was that she would die here. Soon. There was no point in her owning anything.

That particular thought started leading her brain down a bumpy road full of sadness—how her family would react, what would happen to Roen...

Don't, Liv. You've been to this rodeo before. There's no time or room for sulking. Just doing. And doing meant knocking down the closest hurdles. One at a time. For the moment, she'd staved off Roen's death. Now they suspected that the men couldn't survive without the water, so it was fortunate that Dr. Fuller had just landed. She knew quite a bit about the sacred water, so she might be able to come up with a solution. *Because you won't be here.* But she'd tell Dr. Fuller to start working on it. They had a lab, several scientists— mermen, of course—and a Harvard doctor on the island, all of whom probably knew more than anyone but were too weak to work. At a minimum, Dr. Fuller could coordinate.

"That's a discussion for another day." Roen began to get up, wincing as he moved.

"Dammit, merman. You will stay here. You will

rest. You will do as you are told," she barked.

Roen blinked at her, seemingly shocked. Not that she wasn't normally an opinionated and moderately stubborn sort of woman, but she was no Miss Bossy Britches either. *Well, today I fucking am.*

"Fine," he grumbled, "but don't go anywhere near that ocean and those maids, you understand? And when you get back, we're going to have a long talk about everything—including what happened to Shane, how we're going to deal with this island, and how we're going to build a life together. Is that clear?"

Her heartstrings wound tightly together. He had no clue how much it pained her that they wouldn't get the chance to really be together.

He added, "And then we're going to foke. Hard. I don't care if a goddamned hurricane is on our heads, it's happening."

You bet your sweet manly ass it is. "I need a flashlight."

He jerked his head toward the walk-in closet. "In the dresser—bottom drawer."

She gave him a warm smile and then bolted inside the closet. She grabbed the flashlight and headed out of the room, resisting the urge to just stay there with him and kiss his soft lips for another ten minutes.

She hurried downstairs and out the front door. As she hiked along the dark trail, she started berating herself. *You're being naïve, Liv. You've already given up. You're just assuming there's no way out.*

It wasn't like her one little bit. She was a fighter. She was…

She approached the long dirt runway where the plane sat idle, the lights on the wings blinking away. The stairwell was extended, but there was no one going in or coming out.

The hair on the back of her neck stood straight up. *Something is wrong.* Cautiously, she approached the stairs and was about to climb when she heard a woman scream, and it was a voice she recognized.

"Dana?"

Liv bolted up into the plane.

CHAPTER TEN

Liv wondered if perhaps she'd never survived that storm all those months ago and went down with the fishing boat, somehow landing in hell, where she was being forced to live through one impossible nightmare after another.

Yes, this is definitely hell.

Liv stood in the front of the jet, her back to the open doorway.

To the right, Dana lay cowering in the front seat, blood trickling down her forehead from a small cut. She held an unconscious man wrapped partially in a blanket in her arms. His face was covered with those giant charcoal black splotches, and his arms hung limp to his sides. In the row behind Dana, Dr. Fuller sat shaking like a leaf.

Okay. How the hell did Dana get on this plane? Liv didn't know if she wanted to weep with joy because Dana was alive and sitting just a few feet away, or scream hysterically because, obviously,

Dana was on the fucking plane.

With two strange men pointing guns at everyone.

Where the hell did they come from?

Liv's sat phone buzzed in her pocket, reminding her she hadn't spoken with Phil again. Phil, who'd been trying to warn her of…

Well, of this, obviously. But these were not tourists. And fuckingshithell. Hadn't Phil said something about there being one hundred of them?

Okay. Stay calm. Pretend you knew they were coming, put them on their guard.

"You must be some of the assholes from that ship. We've been expecting you," Liv said to the guy standing in the cockpit to her left, pointing an automatic weapon at one of the pilot's heads.

The middle-aged bald man—husky, sweaty, and dirty—flashed his yellow teeth, giving her a vicious smile. Toward the back galley, another man—wiry frame, dark skin, and even darker eyes—held a gun.

Her mind quickly went to work, trying to pull a solution together. These men had gotten past one of the beaches, which meant the maids were either too weak to fight or they had been no match for guns. Second, they had mermen on this island. Two hundred weak mermen. Most weren't fit to stand, let alone fight. Not without food, more water, and more time. Third, they had about sixty ex-mermaids who were fiercely protective of their men, but they were weak, too. No one had eaten. No one had been sleeping. Their only weapons were knives and machetes.

Dammit. They had only one good option: get

these intruders to leave.

"I know why you're here," she said. "But you've come at a bad time. There's an illness going around on the island." She looked at the man in Dana's arms—likely Roen's other pilot, Ed or Eddie or something—to prove her point.

"He ain't come from the island," the bald guy said.

"He was here a couple of days ago. That's how he caught it," Liv argued, hoping to convince the man that staying was not a good choice.

"Guess it's a nice thing you've got that special water here on the island."

Liv laughed. "You don't really believe that crap, do you?"

The man scowled at her. "I seen it in my dreams. I seen it. The island told me to come and take it."

Liv blinked at him. It was just like with Dr. Fuller. *Just like with you. Just like with Roen.* The island wanted all of this to happen. She'd lured these men here. But why?

"Don't you look at me like that," he growled. "I know this place is special. I know that water is worth a lot of money. It's mine now. The island said so."

Fuck. What the hell was happening?

"Okay," Liv said. "You can have it. But I'm the only one who knows where the water is now."

He pointed his weapon at Liv. "Then you best be tellin' me, lady."

Liv raised her hands in the air a little higher. "I will. For a price," she added. "Let me get the food and medicine off the plane and to all of the sick people."

"You'll take me to that water or you will fucking die."

Liv smiled at him, letting him know that she wasn't afraid. If anything, he should know she was a woman of different cloth. One who didn't back down from bullies and wasn't afraid to die. He had no choice but to negotiate with her.

"This island," she said, "and the people who live here are all connected. If they die, she dies. No more water. It's in your best interest to let this doctor try to help them."

A gunshot echoed off in the distance, jolting Liv in her skin.

The man smiled sadistically. "Better hurry. I think one of your patients just bit the bullet."

Oh no. These guys were going to pick off the mermen in their bungalows one by one.

Another gunshot rang through the air off in the distance.

"Another one bites the dust." The man smiled.

"Fine, Freddie Mercury," Liv blurted out. "I'll take you."

The man gave her a strange, irritated look.

Not a Queen fan, huh?

He looked back at his men. "One of you start going through the cargo hold and see what's down there. We'll be setting up camp here, so we'll be needing any supplies they brought. And kill these people if I'm not back in an hour." He turned his attention to Liv. "Lead the way."

With a gun to her back, Liv glanced over her shoulder and gave Dana a comforting smile. *How the hell had she ended up on the plane?*

It was as if the island had carefully orchestrated this entire event, like a tragic Shakespearean play. Maybe the island wanted revenge on those who'd wronged or disobeyed her, so she'd brought these depraved criminals to torture and kill everyone. But then why had the island made a deal with her? The island asked for her life in return for the water to save the men. And why the hell would the island tell this man about the place, but not tell him where to find the water? *I mean, why stop at just leading him to the shore?*

They were being played and manipulated. There was no doubt.

"Move it, lady," the bald man said.

Liv looked up at the sky—just for a moment— praying for strength and some help. She noticed the sun just coming up. This would make it harder for her to get away and warn everyone. But Amelia knew the plane was here. *Maybe she saw the men.*

"I said move!" The bald man turned his gun around and hit Liv between the shoulder blades, causing her to stumble her way down the stairs.

Wow. I didn't think there could be anything worse than mermen. But for all of their vile, archaic, and ruthless ways, at least they behaved according to *some* rules. They believed that their natural advantages—strength, looks, endurance, and the natural attraction women had for them—were fair play, like a tiger had a right to use its teeth and claws. Yes, that made them opportunistic assholes. But these men were a completely different breed. Monsters. They lived by no codes, they didn't care about anything but their own greed, and they were the sort of men who preyed on the weak. Working in a battered women's shelter had taught her to spot them a mile away.

There would be no persuading them to leave or behave reasonably. She got that now.

"You touch me again," she growled, "and I'll personally feed you to the maids."

He laughed. "And the butlers, too? How about the chauffeur?"

"I'm talking about those creatures on the beach," Liv clarified.

The man laughed. "Yes, those little hermit crabs were scary. Now move your ass," the man said, "or I'll shoot you in the stomach so you die slowly."

They hadn't seen the maids? *Strange.*

Without a word, she turned toward the Great Hall, and it suddenly dawned on her. If Amelia got away, she would go straight to Roen. And Roen would come running, too weak to fight and definitely outnumbered. There were over a hundred of these assholes somewhere on the island.

Shit. She had to do something. Quickly. This was going to be up to her to settle.

CHAPTER ELEVEN

"Where the fuck is the water?" The bald man slapped Liv across the cheek, sending her flying onto the cold stone floor of the Great Hall.

Liv wiped the blood off her mouth with the back of her hand. *Asshole!* "I told you," she said, "the island is sick. There is no more water." These men would see no reason to let anyone live once they had what they wanted, so she wasn't about to tell them jack.

He picked her up by the collar of her T-shirt and slapped her again. She flew back, nearly hitting the carved wood throne. *Motherfucker.*

Leaning forward on both hands, trying to stop the room from spinning, Liv opened her eyes and that was when she noticed a rusty machete lying underneath the chair. *Oh my God.* It was just one reach away. But if she rushed this guy, he could easily stop her.

Get him closer, Liv. If she could surprise him, she could land a blow.

She twisted her body onto her butt with her legs straight out and her arms extended behind her. Her right hand was now only a foot from the machete. "Well, since you seem to want me on the floor, I'll just stay here."

The rage in the man's face was nothing shy of lethal. "You said you'd take me to the water," he growled.

"This is where the water comes out. But we have an island full of sick men. Don't you think that would be different if we had the water?"

The man's eyes shifted a bit. He wasn't a smart one, but that was usually the case for men who beat women—they used their muscles because their brains were too small to get what they wanted any other way.

Liv looked up at him. "If you think hitting me some more will do any good, be my guest. But if you want water, you'll have to talk to the island."

The man approached and squatted in front of her but was too far for her to make a move and not have him see it coming. *Get closer, asshole.*

"Oh no," she taunted, "what's the matter? Island doesn't want to tell you? I bet your men think you're an idiot. I bet you promised them they'd be millionaires if they just trusted you. You're all a bunch of fucking idiots."

Another gunshot went off somewhere just outside.

The man looked away for a split second, and Liv took her chance, gripping the machete and lunging. She struck him in the shoulder, and he fell back, wailing. She raised the machete and struck him again at the base of his neck. Blood came from the wound as he screamed and pointed his gun at her. She quickly swung again, hitting him in the arm. The gun skidded across the floor.

The man hacked and moaned for all of ten seconds before his eyes rolled into the back of his head. Liv stood there panting, staring down at him as he stopped breathing.

She wanted to retch. It was the bloodiest thing she'd ever seen. This world of theirs, this island, had turned her into a savage just like the mermen. The only difference being that she was fighting for the people she loved, not for Crazy Dirt.

Oh, shit! Dana!

Liv grabbed the gun on the floor and threw the strap over her shoulder, rushing from the Great Hall. She stopped for a moment as the trail forked— one way led to Roen's, the other back through the forest and to the plane.

Roen was in no condition to help, but maybe some of the other men were in better shape. They hadn't been injured like Roen.

"Liv! Liv!" From the direction of Roen's house, Amelia came running down the hill between a stand of dead, orangish brown pine trees, slipping on fallen pine needles.

"Be quiet," Liv hissed.

Panting, Amelia stopped right in front of Liv, doubling over. "Roen went off to the plane to help you."

Oh no. "Their leader made me come here to

show him the water. I just killed him." Liv's mind darted back and forth. Roen was heading to the plane. He was smart enough not to go in with guns blazing. Right? Then again, mermen went a little mer-nuts when their women were in danger.

"Amelia, you have to go and try to warn the others."

Winded, Amelia replied, "Jason said there was some sort of alarm or something. He went to go trigger it."

Liv remembered there was an enormous communication tower over by the harbor. She'd seen it the last time she'd been here. So, of course, they had some way of sounding an alarm.

Amelia went on, "He said that he'll signal for everyone to make their way to the Great Hall. We'll figure out who's strong enough to fight and who stays behind to look after the men who are still weak."

Suddenly, the air filled with the sound of...

"Are those seagulls?" Liv asked.

"I think that's their alarm," Amelia said.

Jesus, it sounded like the soundtrack from that old birds movie. But the recording or whatever only lasted ten seconds.

"Okay," Liv said, "I'm going to see if I can't catch up to Roen. I'll meet you back at the Great Hall." She hoped Amelia wasn't squeamish, because she'd just gone all merman on that horrible man.

"Be careful, Liv," Amelia said as Liv ran off.

As she bolted through the woods, pushing her

body to run as fast as it could, she tried her best to keep an eye out for any of these men. Yes, she now had an automatic gun strapped to her back, but she had no clue how to use it.

When Liv came up to the tree line skirting the runway, she saw that the belly of the plane was open and there were a lot more men now. Maybe a dozen, if not more.

Where the hell is Roen? She could only pray he hadn't tried to get inside the plane.

She looked up at the light blue sky and whooshed out a breath. Going back to the Great Hall was her only choice now.

As she hiked back, she spotted five men heading down the trail toward Roen's house, but they were walking away and didn't see her. Then, as she continued on the path toward the Great Hall, she heard screaming and gunshots up ahead.

Oh shit. Was everyone in there already? It had only taken her ten minutes to get to the runway and about twenty to turn back around because she wasn't sprinting. But if everyone had gathered inside the hall, then what the hell would she do now? She was all by herself. Liv pressed the sides of her head, feeling like she was in some twisted mermen slash pirate version of the *Hunger Games*, the island being the one pushing all of the buttons. Was all this purely for her amusement?

This can't be happening. She was stuck all alone, in the worst possible situation.

Deep voices coming from two different directions startled her. She hid behind a tree, listening to them speak in some sort of Slavic language.

Okay. Think, think, Liv. But that was easier said than done. She hadn't eaten or slept more than a quick nap, and she'd been under insane amounts of stress. Liv moved away from the voices and started heading in the direction of the beach just on the other side of the mountain.

"Where the fuck do you think you're going?" said a voice that came out of nowhere. She turned quickly and saw a thin man with a big gun. She had one, too, but it was hanging off her back.

Liv slowly raised her hands.

The man's gaze settled right on the gun hanging to her side. "Where the fuck is Yohan?"

Yohan. The guy she killed was named Yohan? He'd looked more like a Vlad or a Beavis, but not Yohan.

"I asked you a question." He aimed his gun at her, and in that moment, Liv realized he had every intention of shooting her.

"I found the gun on the trail. I don't know where your Yohan is," she lied. And he knew it.

Liv saw a dark shadow rise up behind him. The thing was at least nine feet tall.

"Holy shit," she whispered, unable to believe the size of the mermaid who was in the process of opening its razor-sharp jaws. The man turned to see what had grabbed Liv's attention just in time for Liv to cover her eyes.

The man didn't even scream. There'd been no time for that. But Liv heard that familiar sound of crunching.

Liv turned to her side and hurled, only there was nothing in her stomach. After a moment, she gathered herself. She needed to get the hell out of there, but when she stood up straight, she realized that the maid behind her wasn't alone.

"Oh, for fuck's sake. This day just needs to end."

❧

Liv didn't know how much time passed—ten, twenty, sixty minutes—but it felt like a slow burn to hell. Every time she tried to get past the maids, they blocked her. She'd run ten yards, there they were. She'd run ten in the opposite direction, there they were again.

They're not going to let me leave. Dozens of yellow eyes blinked like sequenced Christmas lights hiding in the shadows of the dried-out forest all around her.

"Okay." Liv panted, finally giving up. "I get it. I'm going to be your dinner. But there are men— very, very bad men—killing off some of your mates right now as we speak." Liv pointed toward the mountain. "They're killing your sisters, too. Why the hell aren't you eating them? And why the hell did you let those assholes on the island?" Liv's rage, she realized, came from her heart. She had nothing left to lose at this point because she'd already forfeited her life—a debt she'd pay just as soon as the island called it in. But that was the funny thing. Knowing she was, without a doubt, the only person who would and had to die, gave her a certain peace. She no longer felt afraid. Not for herself anyway. She just wanted her life—and her death, she supposed—to mean as much as possible.

The maids didn't move or react.

"I know you understand me," Liv seethed, "way more than you let on. So what do you want?"

That freaking large as hell maid slithered forward, weaving through the fallen branches and a sea of inky black bodies with long tails.

Slowly, the maid stood up on the curve of its tail, towering over Liv nine feet in the air.

Okay, maybe there's a little fear left in me. Liv tried to keep from wetting herself.

It looked down at her as if unsure if it wanted to snack on Liv's head or make her its pet. "Water," it said in a gravelly voice.

"Water?" Had Liv heard her correctly?

The thing lowered its head, putting them nose to nose. Liv could feel its breath on her face, she could smell the salt of the ocean on its skin, she could hear the low, menacing growl deep inside its chest.

"No water. No protection." The maid's bright golden yellow eyes snapped shut and then opened again.

Ohmygod. They wanted water. That was why they hadn't fought. They were…they were… "This is extortion."

The maid's mouth curled into a vicious smile before it slowly nodded.

Liv's first reaction was anger, but she quickly realized that out of everyone here, these women had suffered the longest. The men fought, the men died, but the maids lived on, hoping and praying for the day they'd be released from their hell. The island never saw a reason to let them go or let them move on.

They're fighting. They're standing up for themselves. And Liv simply couldn't blame them.

"You want to be turned back, don't you." Not a question.

The beasts howled and screeched into the air. Liv covered her ears to shield them from the excruciating sound. But it made plenty of sense, and now Liv knew what she had to do.

"The water is there inside the mountain, underneath the floor," Liv said, "but those men are here to take it. If you help us, I'll do everything I can to get you water."

The maid hissed at Liv like a cobra, and she was sure the thing was about to kill her.

Liv was too scared out of her frigging skull to scream. Perhaps a little pee came out, though. *Holy crap.*

The thing ran its pink tongue over its sharp teeth. "We eat bad men. You get water."

Liv sighed with relief. "Thank you. Can you help my sister, too? She's on that plane."

The thing nodded at one of the maids, who slithered off back toward the beach. The rest turned down the path in the direction of the runway. One by one, the maids, about eighty or ninety of them—

Liv was too freaked out to count—followed along, slithering past as if she were invisible.

Liv looked up at the early morning sky, trying to keep it together. *Thank you. Ohmygod, thank you.*

She was about to follow after the horde of creatures but heard gunshots back in the direction of the hall. Her body tensed.

She glanced down the trail leading back to the plane. She wanted to go to Dana, but she knew in her heart that wasn't where she was needed. She was armed now with an automatic gun she'd taken off the leader. No, she had no clue how to use it, but those vile men didn't know that. She had to stop them from killing more people.

Liv charged back up the hill toward the hall and toward the sound of the gunfire. When she reached a small clearing just outside the mouth of the enormous cavern, she spotted the thugs standing in front of a line of mermen and their women. They were shooting them one by one, demanding sacred water.

Liv's heart sank. How could people be so, so cruel?

She came up behind them and pointed the weapon. "Step the fuck back."

One of the men, a toothless bastard with one arm, laughed and then pointed his gun right at one of the women. To the woman's credit, she just glared at him. She wasn't afraid to die. She wasn't going to cower. And she'd probably be the first to jump on the man and fight that gun out of his hand.

Liv heard a loud rustling behind her, branches

snapping, leaves crushing, gravel and dirt grinding. She didn't have to turn around to see what was coming through the forest; the looks on the faces of the men said everything.

"What the fuck are those?" one of the men croaked.

Liv smiled. "Welcome to El Corazón, assholes." The moment those words left her mouth, a wave of hungry maids rushed past her.

಄

It took the maids less than a few minutes to kill all of the men inside the hall and drag them off into the forest along with the dead.

Waste not, want not. Liv tried to feel something, some sort of regret or remorse for those vile men, but it was like the time she killed Shane; she only felt relief. In addition, she felt angry that these thugs had killed some of the maids and the women and men. More than anything, she felt utter disdain for the island. In her heart, she knew that none of this had to happen, but Crazy Dirt had gone out of her way to ensure it did for reasons known only to her.

"Liv!" Roen emerged through the woods, a look of relief on his face. "Where have you been?" He kissed her hard.

"Killing things. Where have you been?"

"I was watching the plane, waiting for those men to finish unloading and leave so I could get in there."

He must've been hidden in another spot, because she hadn't seen him.

"What the hell happened to your face?" he snarled.

"I'm fine," she said. "I promise." Roen's beautiful, normally olive skin, however, was red. His brow was covered in sweat and he looked like he might fall over.

"You sweet, sweet man." She looked up at him and cupped his beard-covered cheek. "But you're in no shape to fight anyone."

Utter adoration shimmered in his exotic-colored eyes as he beamed back at her. "You think that matters?" He gave her a quick kiss, and if it weren't for two things, she would be jumping him. One, she was covered in sweat and blood—so not sexy. And she needed to find her sister.

"Roen, where's my sis..." She turned her head and spotted Dana and Dr. Fuller coming up the path.

"Liv!" Dana yelled.

"You're okay. Thank God, you're okay." She covered her mouth, trying not to cry.

Liv rushed to her sister and hugged her, her heart swelling and weeping with joy. Dana wasn't just her younger sister, she felt like her child in some ways. Liv had helped raise her.

Liv gripped her sister's shoulders. "How the fuck did you get on that plane, and where the hell have you been all this time?"

Dana, who had long brown hair and big brown eyes, looked like a younger version of herself.

"After Roen and Lyle got me on the plane home, Edward, the pilot, started getting sick. He had these spots all over his face, so we couldn't land at any major airports—they'd haul him away to some lab or Ebola facility."

"Where'd you go?" Liv asked.

"We landed on some private strip in Oregon. I left Edward on the plane and got a car rental. We drove back to Seattle."

"Why didn't you call me or Mom and Dad? Everyone's worried sick about you," Liv asked.

"And risk my call being traced and Edward being seen? Uh-uh. Promised I'd help him get back to Seattle and get a hold of one of the other pilots so we could get him back here where there's water."

"Are you and he?" Liv knew Dana was really into mermen. Big time. She was not immune to their charms.

"No. I promised to help him. He's a nice person."

Howls and screams echoed through the air, interrupting their conversation.

"Liv, what is happening out there?" Roen had been standing beside them as they had their frantic but joyous reunion.

"I got the maids to take care of our intruders," Liv replied.

"Excuse us for a moment," Roen said to Dana and then pulled Liv aside. "You did what?"

"It's fine, Roen. They're not into Liv-meat, for whatever reason. They actually saved me from one of those assholes who was about to shoot me. Then

I promised them what they wanted: water, so they could be turned back."

Roen was clearly struggling to understand her very, very outlandish story. "Do you know where the water is?"

She sighed. "I do, but the island will punish me if I tell, and I'm pretty sure that means what she'll really do is kill you." She looked at her sister. "Or Dana."

"Okay." He rubbed his forehead exasperatedly. "We'll have to figure something out, but you've already saved us all—my brave, brave woman." He kissed her softly and then someone cleared their throat.

They both turned their heads. A large group of men and women had gathered around, including Lyle, Amelia, and a few others she recognized.

"We truly do owe you," said Jason, the blond merman who'd once been loyal to Shane. "My heart will be forever in your debt." He bent down on one knee.

The other men and women all knelt, too. Liv was speechless.

"I'm...uh...thank you?" she whispered. She didn't know what else to say. She simply did what had to be done.

Liv looked at the doctor, who stood in awe of these men. These huge, huge mermen, who'd looked like they'd been through a meat grinder.

"Dr. Fuller, can you start helping these men? Whatever you can do?"

Holden, the island's doctor, wandered up,

bleeding from a giant hole in his arm. "I got shot, but the maids saved me."

Christ. "Start with that one," Liv said. "He's a doctor, too. Dana, can you help her?"

Dana nodded. "Where are you going?" Liv noticed Dana still wore the same black dress she'd had on four or five days ago. She, too, had been running from one fire to the next for days now.

"I'm going to get Roen to his bed," Liv replied. "I'll come check on you soon. And don't wander off anywhere alone. Some of those men are still out there."

"I will keep an eye on her," said a deep voice. It was Lyle. The man looked like he'd seen better days but was in better shape than Roen. Probably because he wasn't recovering from massive blood loss.

Dana looked horrified as she craned her neck, looking up at the shirtless behemoth bulging with muscles and battle-scarred skin. Of course, he was a merman, so he was still insanely beautiful—nice lips, strong jaw, high cheekbones, and hypnotic green eyes—but Lyle had one hell of a scowl and feared nothing. Dana would definitely be safer with him.

"Thank you, Lyle, I appreciate it. Come, you," she said to Roen, intending to do one thing and one thing only: She was finally going to be with the man she loved. Because her gut told her at any moment, the island was going to beckon her to that cave and demand she make good on their agreement. And she would have no choice but to go.

Fucking island. She played a mean game of chess. Including making sure that Dana was back. Between her little sister and Roen, the island knew Liv wouldn't dare double-cross her.

CHAPTER TWELVE

While Roen showered to remove the caked-on blood from his shoulder and hair, Liv lit a log in the stone fireplace in his room to take the chill from the air. The dark wood floors and stoic ceiling mural of a lonely mermaid perched on a rock, gazing out across the ocean, gave the space a peaceful, quiet feel. She could easily imagine Roen sitting in his armchair, staring into the fire, his heart heavy with concern over how to overcome the impossible hurdles inherent to this island.

She then dragged Roen's mattress back up onto the bedframe, changed the sheets, and pulled off her dirty T-shirt. Although she'd already washed her hands and face, she fully intended to shower with Roen. Until she got one look from the doorway of his marble-everything bathroom and couldn't stop watching.

"Wow." Roen was nothing short of godlike in his masculine beauty. Lean sinewy muscles, olive skin, strong arms, and broad shoulders. *Don't forget that ass. The man has a perfect round hard ass.*

He shut off the water and turned around.

"And wow again." She didn't know which part she enjoyed looking at more, his long thick cock hanging between his strong thighs or the deep rippling grooves of his amazing six-pack.

"Are you going to stand there gawking at my mermanliness or come help me towel off?" He glanced down at his cock, his stunning eyes twinkling with seductive mischief.

She grinned. Even though she knew he was far from healed and this situation was far from over, they needed this moment together. They'd been through so, so much and had fought so hard to keep each other alive and safe that they'd never had the chance to really *be* together.

Suddenly, a rush of nerves flooded Liv's entire body. Pre-sex jitters.

"I could stand here forever looking at you," she said, "but you really should get back to bed." She grabbed a towel from a hook on the wall and carefully blotted the healing wound. She then reached for the top of his six-six frame to dry his hair, which was now jaw length and a bit darker than before but still had those golden highlights from the sun.

Standing so close to his large, naked body, the smell of his freshly washed skin instantly made her body ache.

She toweled off the rest of his chest, and he gently placed his hand over hers. "You're amazing, Liv."

She gazed into his eyes for a moment but had to break away. She didn't want him to see that this moment was leading up to goodbye. "Thank you."

"No, really. You humble me with your braveness."

She shrugged. "It was nothing. I just got the maids to fight for us."

"I heard you killed their leader, Liv. That couldn't have been easy."

"He wasn't my first this week."

A certain look of knowing flashed across his face. "So you did kill Shane."

She nodded. "He told me that you were all dead and that he and I would repopulate."

Roen frowned. "He's lucky he can only die once because I'd like to kill him all over again."

"He said the island chose me, Roen."

"Shane was crazy. The island is crazy. The only thing that makes sense in this place is you and me." He reached for her hand and slid it over his heart.

"What's going to happen to all of you now? That water wasn't enough to keep anyone going for long."

He nodded. "It seems that we all have a connection to this place we cannot break. But I know my men, and while some may be bastards, unmated or mated, loyal or lost in this world, we all have one thing in common: We'd all rather die than continue living like this. If nothing else, for our children's sakes, many of whom are already out there in the world and will be summoned to relive the pain of every man who's ever come to this place." His grip on her hand tightened. "This way of life has to end, Liv."

Her eyes filled with tears. "So you're saying you don't care if there's no more water."

"I care about leaving you behind. Just like the men who've had their women returned to them care. Very deeply. But I am prepared to die if it means the island will die too and end this torment."

She understood how he felt. It was just kind of fucked up how everyone was running around falling on swords, when really only one "person" needed to go away.

"And what do you think about this folklore that says she's the spark of all life?"

"It has to be a hoax. I cannot see how something so evil is responsible for bringing life into this world, can you?"

No. She couldn't. "Then what is she?"

"I don't know," he said quietly, mulling it over. "But something so cruel, who seems to thrive off of the suffering of others, can only bring pain into this world." Roen began to wobble a bit.

"Let's get you off your feet." She helped him back into the bedroom over to the bed. "She's powerful, Roen. Whatever she is, she won't go without a fight."

He slid under the covers and Liv couldn't help noticing that Roen was slightly aroused. Then there was this buzzing sensation she felt when she touched him—a merman thing.

A horny merman thing.

It was difficult for either of them to be in the

same room and not want each other, even if they were having a serious conversation or in the middle of a disaster, which, she realized, was every minute they'd ever been together. They'd never known a moment of peace or the joy of simply being a couple who desperately loved each other.

"She may fight all she likes," he said. "It won't change a thing: We're done being her slaves. We're done taking orders from her. If that means we die, then we die." He adjusted himself on the bed and winced. "I'm just foking glad I didn't turn into a mermaid."

Liv made a little laugh. "That would've been scary; although, I think you'd look kind of hot with a tail."

He grinned. "Well, I think you would be lovely with giant fangs and big yellow eyes. Perhaps I will bite you."

"I don't know, Roen. Those ladies have some pretty weird anatomy going on down there." She leaned in to whisper, "I don't think they actually have vaginas. But I do kind of like their knockers— very Goth."

He chuckled. "Only you could make me laugh at a moment like this. You truly are an amazing woman, Liv. I couldn't be a luckier man, even if our days were always numbered."

She wanted to lash out at his defeatist attitude, but he spoke the truth.

She sighed and then gazed into those warm green eyes with golden rings around the pupils. She could stare at him all day, drinking in his masculine beauty. The curves and hardness of his chest. The ropes of hard muscles that ran down his arms. The deep ripples of his abs.

Okay. Enough looking. She needed him and had since the moment they'd met. She wouldn't let yet another opportunity to be with him pass her by.

She leaned forward and touched her lips to his. The warmth of his mouth and the scent of his skin infused her mind with so much emotion, so many decadent sensations. They were luckier than most, she realized, despite the insanity and brevity of their time together. The powerful connection between them was soul-shatteringly good.

She ran her hands down the sides of his face, enjoying the coarseness of his short beard. Not breaking the kiss, she moved her body and straddled his lap. She slid her tongue between his teeth and tasted him slowly. She always found something about Roen so addictive. From the first moment she heard that voice and saw that strong frame of his, she knew she wanted him. The way he looked at her, fought for her, and protected her over and over again made her heart open right up to him. To know that sort of love from a man was nothing shy of magical. And now, as he kissed her, their mouths moving together in a hedonistic dance of licks and sucks, every move was evidence of how perfectly attuned they were to each other.

Roen ran his hands up the sides of her waist and over her breasts, massaging her through her bra. Liv rocked her hips, grinding herself into his now hard shaft waiting for her underneath the sheet.

She was already so wet for him. "God, Roen. I will never get enough of you," she whispered between blazing hot kisses.

He cupped her cheeks and stared into her eyes. "Nor I you."

She felt like tearing up again, but she wouldn't dare let anything get in the way of this. She slid off him and stood to the side of the large bed. She then stripped off her bra, and then, staring into the eyes of the man she loved more than her own life, she slid down her shorts and panties.

The hard lust in his gaze ignited a fire deep in her core. The way he wanted her, the way he fucked her with his eyes was pure sin. And she loved every bit of it.

She peeled back the sheet covering his cock. He was hard and long and thick and so…

Perfect.

She crawled onto the bed, straddled his lower legs, and leaned forward to lick the tip of him. Roen threw back his head and groaned as she tasted him and savored every velvety inch. Seeing him losing his mind from pleasure was the world's greatest aphrodisiac.

She rose up and moved to straddle him, positioning him at her wet and needy entrance. "Roen, I love you." She slowly sank down onto him, watching as every pulsing inch of his hard flesh slid deliciously inside her. "Oh God, you feel so good." The way he filled her completely was unlike anything.

She raised herself, leaving only the tip of him

inside, and sank down again, gripping the firm muscles of his pectorals to steady herself.

He groaned again, in a deep, throaty voice. "Fuck, Liv. You're going to make me come too fast."

He had no idea how sexy he was and what he did to her heart. *I can't stand to leave him. Not again. Dear God, not again.*

Don't think about that, Liv. Be here. Right now. Just him and you and nothing else.

"That's the point, merman. To make you come." She wanted him to lose his mind for her. There was no bigger turn-on.

Roen suddenly shifted and threw her down onto her back, pinning her arms over her head. "God, Liv. I love you." He thrust hard, stealing her breath. "You deserve a thorough fucking."

"O-o-okay…" she stuttered and then whooshed out a breath. The weight of his body and powerful muscles bracing her was sinful. He lowered his mouth to hers, kissing her and breathing into her as he pumped and she tried not to orgasm. All she could think of was how well they fit and felt and moved. Like one soul and two halves. *More. I want more.*

But he was too perfect. The way he throbbed inside her, the friction just right against her c-spot. It was like he read her mind and body and everything, knowing just what she needed.

Quickening his pace, pumping vigorously, Roen slid one hand down to cup her breast and his lips journeyed down her neck.

She wanted to make this moment last until dawn, but the truth was he had an instant effect on her. "I'm close. I can't…" She exhaled. "Wait."

Roen slid one hand underneath her head and the other under her hip. "We will spend every moment together, until my last breath, doing nothing but this." He kissed her. "Just come for me."

She stared into his eyes, hoping he wouldn't see the truth: This was it for them. Meanwhile she tried to absorb and cherish every fleeting second. Them. Together. Joined. Nothing else.

She exploded, throwing her head into the pillow and digging her nails into his back, screaming his name.

He unleashed his passion, holding nothing back, pounding his cock into her. The rawness of his movements only elevated the intensity of her orgasm. Suddenly, he froze, leaning deep with his hips, his long thick cock hitting that magical spot, sparking another orgasm.

"Oh God, Roen," she moaned. Then she felt his teeth grabbing her shoulder—something mermen instinctually did with their mates—but this time she didn't care. Liv didn't flinch. She knew he'd never really hurt her. He'd walk through the fires of hell before he'd harm a hair on her head. His love for her stronger than his urges.

His mouth clamped down as he came hard, shuddering with every ejaculation inside her.

Several moments passed as her body floated down from the high of connecting with this man so passionately, so wholly.

He collapsed on top of her, and though she could barely breathe, she wouldn't trade one shallow breath in this moment for anything. His heart pounded against hers, his rough beard scraping her collarbone, his legs intertwined with hers while they remained connected.

She smiled to herself and ran her hand over the back of his soft damp hair, silently thanking the universe for giving her this moment. So much happiness.

"*Liv, it's time now*," said that sadistic female voice.

Liv's blissful daze evaporated. What? *Fuck. No. No. Not yet. Just one more minute.*

"*Come to me, human. Do not make me ask twice.*"

CHAPTER THIRTEEN

Liv listened to the sound of Roen's deep breaths as he rested tightly pressed against the length of her body. With tears in her eyes, she carefully slid from the bed and found a piece of paper and pencil on his dresser among a stack of old books he'd been studying.

She jotted down a note, hoping Roen for once in his life would listen.

Please know that I wouldn't change a second of my life because I got to share my heart with you. Don't ever doubt that.

I love you.

Liv

She placed the sheet of paper on top of the books, right where he would see it.

"Clock is ticking, human," said the island.

Liv had hoped for more time, but that wasn't going to happen.

She looked over her shoulder, taking one last look at the beautiful man in the bed before making her way downstairs, through the kitchen and then down the dark stairwell to the basement. She looked at the narrow tunnel, shaking like hell. She didn't want to die. She didn't want the island to win, but she was not willing to risk the lives of those she loved who'd be punished if she took one misstep.

Liv took a steadying breath and crawled into the damp dark tube. With every inch closer, the temperature of the air grew colder. She felt the steam of her breath across her nose.

Finally, a small glow of green light shined at the end of the tunnel. She was freezing cold, her fingers stinging as she used her hands to guide the way. When she reached the small cavern, the water in the pool appeared a thousand times dimmer. At least the bodies were gone. Had they sunk to the bottom, or had this creature devoured them?

"Okay. I'm here, Crazy Dirt. Let's make this quick." Just because the island was powerful and mysterious, didn't mean Liv had to be polite. She hated her. She hated everything about her. A fucking bully. A greedy, heartless tyrant.

"Crazy Dirt? You dare insult me?" she said.

Liv laughed. "I can call you Dirty Fucking Bitch if you prefer."

"Now, now, human. No need to be uncivilized."

"Oh, but there is a need; it makes me feel better. So tell me what you want me to do? Hop on in so you can suck the life from me?"

The island laughed. *"I had something more*

interesting in mind."

She probably wants to watch me suffer first. "Whatever you do to me won't matter. Roen and his men are through. They don't care if they die. They won't ever bow down to you again. They won't lift a finger to save you, even if it means they all perish."

"Oh, my dear human—"

"Liv. My name is Liv. As in…I will and you won't. Not without those mermen to feed you."

"I don't need them to worship me anymore—I just need you. It's like Roen once told me, those who don't evolve don't survive. And it's time for me to take the next step in my journey."

What the hell was she talking about?

Suddenly, the water from the pool began to rise in the shape of a body resembling Liv's, glowing a bright green.

"What the…" Liv's voice faded as a watery hand extended and punched right through Liv's chest.

Liv wanted to scream from the pain, her legs wanted to give out, but this thing had wrapped itself around her heart. It held her in place as it squeezed.

"Where's that smartass mouth of yours now, human? Huh?"

Liv gasped for air and tried to claw at the arm reaching into her body, but her hands went right through it.

"Oh yes, Liv. I can feel it now; your heart is strong. Your heart will feed me for a very, very long time."

Liv prayed for the pain to stop, for the island to

finish her off. She'd never felt anything so terrifying and agonizing. "Let. Me. Die," Liv croaked.

"Die? Dear no, human. It's just like you said; you will live. You will live here forever. What do you think all of this was for?"

Liv watched as the arm pulled back, ripping her heart from her chest. There was little blood, but as it tore away, she felt her soul going with it.

What was happening? She cupped her hands around her heart, instinctively fighting for it, not wanting to let it go. Her love for her family, for Roen, for life…it was all slipping through her fingers.

She lost her grip as her body fell onto the cold wet ledge next to the pool. She watched helplessly as her heart disappeared into the pool and the water began to grow brighter.

Liv couldn't move. Her body began to go numb. Her lungs couldn't breathe.

"I fucking hate you," Liv gasped, tears running down her face.

"That's too bad, human, because you and I will be connected for a very long time."

Liv watched as that watery shape reached inside itself and pulled out a swirling liquid ball. Before Liv could process, that hand shoved itself into her chest again.

Liv's lungs expanded, and she heard a heartbeat so loud, it stung her ears. Liv screamed at the top of her lungs and then passed out.

꒰꒱

When Liv woke, it was with a horrified gasp. Her first reaction was to believe it had all been a nightmare, but as she placed her hand over her chest, the spot felt tender. She slowly sat up and stared at the water to her side glowing bright green.

"*What did you do to me*?" she said.

There was a loud sigh. "To us, Liv. I did it to us."

"*What*!" she screamed. "*What did you do*?"

"Do you have any idea how long I've waited for this? To feel air in my lungs, to feel the sun on my face, to be able to leave this place."

"*What did you do!*" Liv yelled again.

That was when Liv realized she couldn't hear the sound of her words coming from her mouth or ricocheting off of the cold stone walls. When the island spoke, however, the sound was clear. The sound was her own voice.

"Oh my God. You…you…took my body?"

"That's right, human. Now you're catching on. We've switched places."

Holy crap. That wasn't just their hearts she'd swapped; it had been their souls.

She went on, "You and I are now connected, Liv; but your soul is anchored to this hellhole and I am anchored to your body. Of course, my watery heart still needs this place to exist, which means the island must be well fueled. But you, Liv—" she chuckled "—your heart is strong enough for both of us. Well, you and the mermen you're now connected to. I think their love for you was just the added boost I needed to pull myself away and crawl into my new home. So thank you for that! They really, really adore you," she said cheerily.

"*But...how? How is this possible?*" Liv asked out of shock as much as she did for her own knowledge. She couldn't let this happen.

"I've been watching you, Liv, since the moment I tasted your life. I hoped you'd be the one to free me."

"*This was your plan all along?*"

"Well, of course, I had to test your strength to make sure you wouldn't die on me like the others who've come before you. But to my utter delight, the more I tested you, the stronger you became. Separating you and Roen, watching you fight for your sister's life and for your own, killing Shane, all of those were in the name of making you stronger, preparing you for this day. I wanted your heart as strong as possible, and now...not only do I have the mermen's hearts open to me again—via you, of course—but I finally have what I've wanted for as long as I can remember: a body."

I have to warn Roen. She tried to move her body, but couldn't. Yet she could still sense a strong connection.

The water rushed into the small cavern, rising like a vicious tide. Liv felt her body sweeping away, being pulled under. The glowing green water was all around her, in her lungs, in her nostrils and ears. And in the space where her heart once was.

No, no, no. This can't be happening.

She felt her body rising up and then falling. When she opened her eyes and looked around her, she was on the floor of the Great Hall. The walls dripped with water; the pools filled again.

Liv's body staggered to its feet, lungs gasping for air. She felt these things happening, but she wasn't controlling any of it. Her gaze then dropped to her trembling hands, hands that had moments ago held her own heart.

Crazy Dirt was soaking in the joy of being able to touch and breathe, while the only thought in Liv's mind was this was too insane to be real. But it was real. And this had been the island's plan all along. Crazy Dirt knew her end was coming. She knew the ride was over. And she'd found another way to survive and get what she needed.

"Roen will never be fooled by you. He knows me," Liv croaked.

"He's an idiot. And he'll believe whatever I tell him to. Just like all of the other mermen on this island."

"Liv!" Roen's heavy breaths echoed in her ears.

Liv again felt her body moving, almost like she was inside herself, watching via a spy camera. She could even see Roen through her own eyes.

Oh, God. I've gone insane.

"Roen!" she heard her own voice say, but it was really Crazy Dirt speaking. "The island surrendered. You can save your men and the maids."

"Woman, what happened to you?" Roen asked.

That's right, Roen. Don't fall for it. She's not me. She's not me.

CHAPTER FOURTEEN

Roen had woken up feeling sore, tired, and completely sated. Having sex with Liv left him tapped out. It had also left him without words. In his old life, he had been a different man. One whose only real ambition was making money and building his company. He had valued the people in his life for what they could do to serve his own wants and desires.

Women were no exception.

He appreciated their beauty and how good they made his dick feel. He also appreciated how quickly they left after he fucked them. But, as Liv once pointed out, they'd used him, too. They each had their own reasons—prestige, pleasure, whatever— but not one had ever cared enough about him to see him as a person. They never called. Never fought to keep him. They were happy with one night, perhaps too intimidated by him to ask for more or too frightened of what they might find when the fantasy of Roen Doran evaporated, leaving behind a real

man of flesh and bones. A man with flaws and
darkness in his heart. Not that he cared about them
or what anyone thought. Not that he care that his
heart was so thick with scars that he lacked any real
feelings or warmth whatsoever.

But Liv had not only seen what was in his heart,
she'd fought for his life the first day they'd met.
Her braveness humbled him. Would she ever
understand that? Would she ever comprehend how
she was ten times stronger than him? Her spirit, her
resolve, her heart—she was a warrior of another
breed. That was why his people had all kneeled for
her. Out of sheer respect for her spirit.

He'd never thought it possible to see these
men—ruthless, fearless, unafraid to die or kill—
bow to a woman. But they had. A human one at
that. They loved her. They felt honored by how
she'd put herself at risk for them and their mates
while asking for nothing in return. Hell, even he
wasn't that selfless. He always wanted something:
their obedience, their loyalty. But she'd asked for
nothing.

And now that he and Liv had finally
consummated their love, it had become far more
difficult for him to accept his fate. Did he really
have to die with this island? Why did it have to end
like this?

As he'd pushed his cock into her, feeling her
sweet warm body beneath his, clinging to him,
moaning his name as he came inside her, his only
thoughts were of wanting more time. Not just for
fucking—though that certainly would be nice—but

for them to be happy. *This can't be all there is for us. It can't be.* But Liv's breath and soft touches soothed his aching soul and brought him back into the moment with her. Just her. Then he drifted off into a blissful sleep.

When he woke to an empty space beside him, terror flooded his mind. He could hear Liv screaming for him. He could feel her anguish.

"Liv! Liv!" He pried himself out of bed, grabbed his suede and a machete, and ran, following the sound of her voice.

Like a dream, he followed the cries drifting in the wind to the Great Hall. "Liv! Where are you?" Then the screaming stopped, and there she was, standing at the center of the large cavern. The walls were flowing with water again, and she was smiling at him.

"Woman, what the foke happened to you?" he asked, still on his guard.

"Nothing. But we won." She glowed with joy. Her skin was radiant with sweat and water. "We did it!" She threw her arms around his neck and kissed him hard.

He pulled her back, gripping her by the shoulders. "Why were you screaming?"

"That fucking bitch of an island tried to hurt me. She tried to convince me to drown myself in the water. But I'm too strong for her, Roen. She's given up. She knows that fighting us won't change anything."

The island surrendered? "Liv, that can't be. She's..."

Liv slapped him hard across the cheek, indignation burning in her eyes. "Roen, wake the fuck up! She needs protection. That's what this was always about. It's over. You're free. I'm free. Why can't you just be happy?"

"Did you just slap me?" he growled.

Liv shrugged. "Sorry. But I don't want to waste a minute. We just got our happy ending, Roen! She gets that she needs our help. Those fucking thugs were proof."

It made sense, but... "What did she say she wants?"

"Exactly like you proposed to her." Liv pushed herself up on her tiptoes and ran her sweet, wet tongue over his lips. "You make sure there are always a few mermen here at all times. You hire that security firm to protect her from intruders. Everyone's happy." Liv gripped his arms, digging hard into his skin with her nails. "You can rotate the men. They can all have lives. You've succeeded, baby." She kissed him again.

He felt sick to his stomach. He leaned over, bracing his arms on his knees. "I need...I need to rest."

He couldn't think straight. This was all too...too...easy. But really, had it been? When he thought of everything they'd endured to get to this point? No, it had been a living hell.

Liv ran over to the now flowing pool of water and scooped some into her hands. She ran back to him. "Drink, Roen. Drink."

He pushed her hands away. "What are you doing?"

Her gaze thickened with anger. "For fuck's sake, Roen. Why do you always have to be so stubborn? Drink the damned water. If I had any doubts whatsoever, I'd tell you. But now you're being delusional. Get well. Then we can heal everyone, give the men back their women, and decide together who stays or goes." She shook him. "It's over, Roen."

She was right. He'd been in fight mode for so long, he simply didn't know how to believe that their luck had turned.

He gave her a quick kiss. "Your lips are cold."

"Then hurry the hell up and get them warm, merman." She flashed a seductive smile.

He strolled over to the pool and bent down. Somehow it felt wrong to drink, but he wanted this, more time with Liv. He wanted it more than life itself.

He drank several gulps, and it was unlike anything he'd ever experienced before, like his soul had been filled with hope and strength. He felt…fucking powerful.

He shook his head from side to side.

"Roen?" Liv grabbed his arm. "Are you okay?"

"Never better." He kissed her and ignored the chill of her lips. Perhaps she was simply in need of a little more kissing.

"I'll get the others," she said excitedly.

"No." He grabbed her elbow and yanked her back. "I'm going to fuck you. Right here. Right now."

His cock felt like a steel post that would explode like a bomb if he didn't come.

She grinned. "Yes, sir. But make it quick, honey. The people await us."

He backed her up to the wall, ignoring how it now trickled with a steady stream of water, and turned her around, yanking down her shorts. He found her entrance and thrust himself into her with one smooth motion.

"Yeah, baby. That feels so good," she moaned.

Why does she feel so cold? Yet, he couldn't stop himself from wanting her. He fucked her hard, focusing on her moans, on the sound of her voice. And when he poured himself into her, all he could think of was that something wasn't right.

Shut the foke up. You just don't know how to be happy.

"Liv!" Dana's voice rang out, and Roen quickly pulled out and covered himself.

Still panting and bracing herself against the wall, Liv grumbled something underneath her breath and then put her shorts back on.

Dana appeared in the doorway of the Great Hall, her eyes lighting up. "Holy shit. What happened in here?"

"The island is healing," Liv said, sounding mildly annoyed. "What do you want, Dana?"

Dana shook her head from side to side. "Oh. Yeah. Um, you guys have to come and see this."

"We're busy, sister. What is it?" Liv responded coldly.

Of course, he didn't appreciate surprises either. He never had. He never would. That said, Liv seemed like she couldn't be bothered.

She's been through a lot, man. She's likely reached her threshold for stress.

"Dana?" he said. "What is the matter?"

Dana blinked up at him, and then she grinned. It was a smile that reminded him so much of Liv. "You're not going to fucking believe this."

CHAPTER FIFTEEN

"I don't foking believe it." Roen ran his hands over the top of his head and stared down at the sleeping creature—clearly male—lying on the bed in the modest bedroom. The doorway began filling up with curious faces—the maids who'd been transformed. Word always spread quickly on this island.

Dana, who stood behind Roen, peeked around him and looked at the thing on the bed. "I watched it happen. I was holding his hand, and he died. At least, I thought he did. And then it just happened."

Roen looked at Dana. "This is Edward?" Yes, this was Edward's bungalow, but...that was...well, it was a foking merman sleeping on that bed.

Dana nodded, grinning from ear to ear.

"Why are you so happy?" he asked.

She shrugged. "I thought he was dead. Now he's not."

Roen's mind began sliding all of the pieces into place. The water on this island was what transformed them into human-looking creatures. If they ceased taking the water, they returned back to…mermen? However, if a maid drank the water, it healed her from whatever was in their saliva that transformed them.

It was very…interesting. Or confusing? He wasn't sure.

He glanced at Liv, who glared at the thing on the bed. "Guess you can't accuse us of being crazy for calling ourselves mermen, can you, Liv?" He elbowed her.

"He's disgusting. Just like the maids."

Roen looked at Edward's charcoal black skin, his body bursting with powerful muscles that were the size of any merman's arms and chest, if not larger. He had a black scaly tail and a black, well-endowed member dangling where his groin once was. His hair had also transformed into thick twisted ropes of seaweed-looking matter, similar to a maid. And, of course, there were the teeth.

"I dunno." Dana shrugged. "I think he looks like a sexy badass—I mean, look at the size of his—"

"Yes. We see it, Dana," Liv snapped acerbically at her sister. "But I also see that he's got teeth. Sharp ones." Liv grabbed Roen's arm and gave it a squeeze. "Thank God the island is healing. We can give him water and turn him back to the way he was." Her big brown eyes pierced him with a warning, as if to say that he dare not disagree with her.

"Of course, Liv. But this is an extremely important revelation. I think we should get the men together and discuss the news of this."

"You're not honestly thinking of letting all of the men turn back into these things, are you?"

Why was Liv being so…foking pushy?

He looked around the room. "Everyone out, please." Edward might wake up soon, and he'd probably be hungry.

Everyone cleared the room, and Roen followed them out, closing the door behind him. "Please spread the word; we are to gather in the Great Hall. Immediately," he said to one of the ladies. "And, Dana, you are to wait just outside. I need to speak with your sister for a moment and you should not be running around this island unaccompanied. By the way, where the foke is Lyle?"

"He's sleeping. But I need to tell—"

"You will do as you are fucking told, Dana," Liv barked.

Dana shrank back. Clearly, she was not accustomed to her older sister speaking that way to her. Frankly, he wasn't accustomed to hearing Liv speak in such a way either.

"Uh-huh…okay." Dana went outside, and he and Liv went into the small living room of Edward's cabin.

"Liv, I feel like you're not telling me something."

She blinked her lovely brown eyes at him. "I don't know what you mean."

"You left our bedroom after we made love. I found you in the Great Hall, and suddenly the water had returned."

"Yeah. That's right."

"Why were you in the Great Hall? What did the island ask of you?" he asked.

"Nothing. She didn't ask anything. I just heard her calling me, and I came. Then she told me to deliver that message since none of you are listening to her anymore."

That sounded much too simple. "I thought you said she tried to drown you."

Liv blinked at him. "Oh, well, she did. But it didn't work. And then she said she was giving up."

So easily? "Tell me exactly what she said, Liv."

"Roen." Liv rolled her eyes. "I just did. There's nothing else. I think you're just paranoid."

"She's foking dangerous, Liv. You and I both know that. And we know she's been lying and manipulating our people for years."

Candidly, however, he didn't understand why. The island had been ensuring the men took the water—like a drug they'd become addicted to that made them bigger and stronger. Almost like a steroid. And when they stopped taking it, they turned into mermen. Of course, he would've expected a merman to look more like the creatures from their folklore—beautiful with tails of greens and blues. That thing was a monster, just like the maids.

Of course, what did he know? This island's historical records and their legends were shrouded in so many myths and lies that it was difficult to sieve any true information from them.

"I simply do not understand," he mumbled,

partially to himself, "why the island would suddenly change her ways and agree to coexist peacefully."

"Maybe there is no reason other than she really does need your protection. And you, hers. Haven't you ever wondered what would've happened to your people if humans knew about you? You would've been hunted to extinction hundreds of years ago. This place is your safe haven. I mean, nature is full of examples of symbiotic relationships, right? Think about those clownfish that live inside of anemones."

Perhaps Liv was right. "But in symbiotic relationships, each species gains something."

"You're the clownfish. You chase away the humans. In exchange, the island offers you shelter from the world."

He was still missing something. The island and his people didn't exactly live in harmony. Their laws had been designed to encourage killing. The island was quick to punish and harm the men if they disobeyed. No, this did not feel like a mutually beneficial relationship. It felt like enslavement. So what did the island really get from them? Was it truly protection from humans?

And what about their folklore? It said that they were once a powerful people who could command the air and water around them. But at some point they'd given all that up. Then they tried to leave and the island used their women as leverage to keep them here. And finally, there was the matter of her water. She claimed, as did their elders, that the world could not survive without it. That everything and everyone would perish. No new life without her spark.

But what if all that gibberish about being necessary to life on the planet was just another lie meant to prey upon their sense of duty and loyalty?

It would explain why, when he proposed to find another way to keep her safe and protect her, without requiring the mermen to stay here, she resisted.

"I think, Liv," he finally said, "that nothing in this place is as it seems. And that the island's real agenda has yet to be revealed."

"So what does that mean?" she asked, sounding irritated.

"I'm not sure. But I will begin with discussing what we've learned with my people."

"Goddammit, Roen! Do you hear yourself? Do you? Fuck them! Fuck this place! It's our time now. You saved them all. They're free. You and I are leaving here, and we're going to start our life together."

"But, Liv, you don't understa—"

"Oh, but I fucking do, Roen. I understand that you almost died. I understand that that crazy bitch almost killed me and my sister. I understand that she tried to have everyone killed by bringing those men here. And I understand that I am through with this place. So either you love me or you don't. You want me or you don't. But I refuse to spend another moment in this hellhole."

The anger in her eyes was palpable, and he understood why. "But if we leave now, what will become of these men and this place?"

"You do as you planned," she snarled. "The island is legally mine now. Those mercenaries are coming to protect it. The men are free to stay or go. The maids can be cured."

"Yes. But if any of us stop drinking the water, we will turn back to our natural state."

"Then we *fucking* bring some water with us and have a supply shipped to wherever we go!" She grabbed both sides of his face and kissed him hard. Again he noticed how her mouth felt cooler than he remembered.

He pulled back. "Your skin is cold. Are you feeling all right?"

Liv slid one hand down his torso, underneath his suede, and began stroking him with her cool hand. "I feel great. But you feel hotter. Must be the water." She began grinding herself against him as he grew hard and ready in her hand. He'd missed her so much he didn't want her to stop. However...

"We have to get to the Great Hall, the men are—"

Liv pushed him back into the small sofa. "They can goddamned wait." Raw lust gleamed in her brown eyes. "I need to feel you inside me again."

She whipped off her top and pulled down her shorts, revealing that patch of dark hair between her legs that he knew would lead him to the sweetest spot. She moved over him and straddled his lap.

"Liv, you're so fucking sexy." He felt blinded by his need for her.

She took his cock in her hands and then

positioned him just right before slamming her body down on him, sheathing his cock deep inside her. He held back a groan as she rode him hard, trying to coax the cum from his shaft.

His mind in an utter state of oblivion, he gripped her hips and rocked himself into her. She felt cool, but still so delicious. "I'm going to get you pregnant, Liv. You know that, don't you?"

"I fucking hope so, Roen. Come for me, merman. Come inside me." Her supple breasts bobbed in his face as she slid him in and out at a ravenous pace.

As his cum exploded into her, he felt a coldness in his heart.

"Roen, no!" Liv's faint voice echoed somewhere inside his head.

"What the *foke* was that?" he said.

He looked at Liv, her head flung back, her chocolate brown hair cascading down her shoulders. "No! Don't stop, Roen. Don't stop."

He blinked, feeling disoriented for a moment. He could've sworn he'd heard her speaking to him not through his ears, but through his heart.

Of course. She is your mate. "I foking love you, Liv," he said.

She smiled and then pulled his lips to hers for a wet kiss. "I know, baby. I can feel it. Now fuck me again."

"With pleasure." A merman could go all night. "But just once more. Then I have to go to the Great Hall and tell everyone we're leaving."

Liv pressed her mouth to his in a punishing kiss.

჻

Every time Liv heard those manipulating lies coming from her own mouth, twisting words so that Roen wouldn't see the truth, Liv's heart grew angrier.

But when Liv felt Roen inside her body, that fucking evil bitch at the helm, making her limbs and muscles move and stroke and kiss and suck, her heart ached with despair. It was torture watching him make love to this other woman. Yes, it was her body. It was her face and her voice.

But it wasn't her.

Why can't he tell the difference? she screamed to herself. *That's not me, Roen!* And now Crazy Dirt wanted him to have babies with her?

They won't be free, Roen. That evil bitch probably has some other plan. That vile, life-sucking demon probably had the next thousand years of her existence all figured out.

"I foking love you," Roen said, and his words felt like a blanket of soothing warm honey being poured over her raw and aching soul. Those words were meant for her.

But then why was he fucking her again? Why wasn't he seeing the truth?

"Roen! No!" she screamed.

"What the foke was that?" Roen said, stopping the rocking movement of his hips.

He heard me. He heard me! Ohmygod! Roen!

But then that evil bitch started screaming, urging him to continue.

Because she heard me, too. Crazy Dirt could hear everything Liv said, couldn't she? The two of them were connected now in almost every way.

Except I'm not an evil demon. "And I won't let you win, Crazy Dirt! I won't let you have him!"

"Yes, Roen. That's it! Just you and me. No one else matters," Crazy Dirt screamed loudly to mask Liv's cries.

"This isn't over, Crazy Dirt. You can't silence me forever." Which got Liv thinking. If Roen left the island, would he still be able to hear her? The island still had some connection to those off the island, but it wasn't the same. She knew that first hand. It was why Crazy Dirt always wanted the men to stay close to her.

So how would she draw energy or feed or whatever it was called from so far away?

She's bringing lunch with her: Roen.

He'd drink the water from here, he'd stay healthy and strong, and she would draw from him.

Liv wanted to vomit. Crazy Dirt had needed two strong people in order to free herself from this place. Her and Roen. Their love, their bond, their strength. She'd chosen them specifically for this. Liv could see that now.

Who could ever have seen it coming?

I have to stop Roen before he leaves. She just wasn't sure how.

CHAPTER SIXTEEN

Is this truly over? Am I really leaving this place? Roen could hardly believe that the moment had finally arrived. It had come at the great expense of those around him, of those who'd come before him, and of those he loved, but he'd done it.

Well, me and Liv. He glanced at her sweet face— those pink lips, the elegant lines of her nose, jaw, and cheekbones. His heart swelled for this woman who'd been brave enough to return for him. Who'd been fearless enough to confront the threats.

And now, she and he would leave here. Together. The island would be well guarded, his people could choose to stay or go, and there would be no more Collections or killing.

His only concern now was the island's motives.

She had not spoken with him or attempted to; however, he'd shut her out of his heart, as had the other men. He had no doubt that eventually she would try to make her comeback, but what good would it do? They now knew they could live without her water, although many would not want to. Just as he did not. He wanted to live as man and woman with Liv—his human mate.

As for the young men and boys out in the world who had yet to discover what they were, he would just have to wait and see. Would these future mermen continue making their way to the island, being drawn by their blood to join their people? Would they instinctively seek out one of their kind on the mainland? No one knew. He only hoped that instinct would guide them somewhere safe before their bodies underwent any changes, which as far as Roen could tell, happened later in a male's life. Something triggered the mermen gene.

One more mystery to be studied about their people. But this was work that now needed to be left to others. Roen had done his part.

The men, who'd now all been given water, and the women who'd been transformed gathered in the Great Hall.

With Liv at his side, Roen looked around at the smiling faces, and it was a moment he'd never forget.

"You know what?" he said. "This is the beginning of a new life. Let's hold the meeting outside, under the blue sky." This cavern held too many bad memories. "In fact, I'm going to ban anyone using it from here on out. We come, we collect our water, we leave."

From the sounds and rumbles of the voices, everyone seemed to agree. They all made their way outside and to a small clearing just down the hill, where they gathered around him and Liv.

"First," he said, "I want to say how grateful I am that we've been given this chance to live freely. And, as I'm sure you've heard by now, the island fooled us men into believing we were dying when in reality, we were merely returning to our natural state. But I want everyone here to know that they have a choice; they do not need to depend on this island any longer. If they choose to be free and live as our ancestors once did, then they will be safe within the waters surrounding the island. Any further out, of course, comes with a risk of being discovered."

Holden, who stood next to Dr. Fuller, raised his hands. "Dr. Fuller and I have been discussing the idea of trying to bring back all of the maids. We'd like to understand which ones are immune to the water and why. We'd also like to see if there are any who remember their lives before they were changed."

Dr. Fuller spoke up. "We'll also need help to change back all of the maids, so they can decide for themselves how they'd like to live."

Roen hadn't really thought about that. It would require many men. "It will take time; however, I suppose I can—"

"Roen, not to interrupt your speech," Liv said politely, "but you've already given so much to this island. Can't someone else be put in charge? Lyle, for example?"

Roen leaned in close, so only she could hear.

"That is an excellent idea, Liv. I'm thrilled my mate is such a smart woman."

He straightened his back. "We'll get through this next phase. Lyle can handle things—"

"Where are you going?" Lyle asked with his deep, gravelly voice.

Roen lifted his chin, knowing his reply might displease some. "Liv and I are leaving, which is the other reason I wanted to gather everyone. Anyone else who wishes to go may come with us. If you are planning to live as a landlover, we will need to make arrangements for water to be sent to you. In any case, for those who remain here, we are going to need new laws and new leadership on the island. I propose that once we get through the next few weeks and have all of the maids returned to their human state, we will work on a new infrastructure. Everyone will have a say going forward. Everyone will have land and a home. Everyone is free to come and go as they please. Until we've worked out the new laws, however, all disputes are to be handled by Lyle. Killing is prohibited except for self-defense, of course. But I suspect we've all had our fill of fighting."

"Roen," Liv interrupted again, "we cannot risk intruders or being discovered. The island is still sacred. We need her to stay healthy if she's going to keep making water for us."

"That all goes without saying." He took her hand and wrapped his fingers tightly around hers. "We will continue our scientific work, studying this place. We'll set up secure means of transport on and off the island by boat and air so that we can bring in supplies when needed and so that people may come and go. But this land will no longer be referred to as sacred."

Liv's fingers squeezed his. "Well, it's still sacred. The water can heal almost anyone from almost any injury. It's pretty remarkable if you ask me." She looked at Dr. Fuller. "Isn't that right, Doctor?"

Dr. Fuller smiled. "I don't know, Liv. After everything I've seen, I'm wondering if she's not just some demonic freak of nature."

Roen could see the anger in Liv's eyes, and her mouth began to express it out loud. "How can you—"

"All right, Liv," he cut her off. "We've all had a trying few days, and I know we're all in need of a little rest."

Pure rage flickered in Liv's eyes and made him pause. But then that glowing, warm smile he loved so much crept across her lips. "You're totally right, Roen. I haven't slept in days." Liv gave his hand another squeeze. "I'd like to go home now, if you're done playing benevolent ruler."

He leaned down and kissed her. "Yes. I'm through. Let's get you home."

࿇

Liv watched through her own eyes as Roen packed up his things, including some of the island's ancient texts. Crazy Dirt, of course, tried to dissuade him from bringing anything back to the mainland, claiming that the distractions of this place would get between them.

Liv screamed and fought and cried and begged, but every time she saw a look in Roen's eyes, some hint of worry or discomfort, there *she* was, distracting him again. "Fuck me, Roen. Fuck me again," Crazy Dirt would beg.

Roen would then flash that cocky smile, unable to deny his mate what they both wanted. It was a nightmare. A horrific nightmare to witness Roen unknowingly betraying her.

He loves you, Liv. He loves you. He's not doing this to hurt you. "Roen! Don't leave. Don't leave the island!"

Crazy Dirt walked into the bathroom, closed the door, and then stared into the mirror, a look of pure evil flickering behind brown eyes that were so familiar, yet so foreign. "Listen, you human bitch, he can't hear you. The only thing you are accomplishing is giving me a fucking headache and pissing me off."

"Ask me if I give a shit. Roen! Roen!"

Crazy Dirt pounded her fist so hard on the marble countertop that the pain made Liv gasp. "You miserable little cunt, keep behaving like an infant, but it will change nothing. If you behave nicely, however, I promise to bring Roen back from time to time for a visit so you can feel close to him again. Maybe I'll even bring your children by for visits." Crazy Dirt circled her hand over her stomach.

Children? "No." Liv wanted to cry.

"With the way your merman fucks and the strength of your body, I'm probably pregnant already." She laughed.

"You—you can't do that. You can't—"

"Oh, but I can, and I will. We'll have dozens of strong, healthy mermen who will serve me obediently for generations."

No, no, no. She couldn't have babies with Roen! They'd be made with her body and her eggs and DNA, but...*they'll have Crazy Dirt for a mother.*

"I'll fucking kill you. I swear to God, I will kill you." Liv was about to lose her mind. Once again, she found herself wondering how any of this was even possible. Her mind and soul now existed in this strange dark place outside her body. A body that she still felt connected to and breathed and walked with Crazy Dirt's heart inside it.

Crazy Dirt shrugged. "You have no hands or real power, so I think I'm safe from you, Liv." Crazy Dirt wiggled her fingers in the mirror. "Ta-ta, little human."

Crazy Dirt walked out of the bathroom and went to find Roen. He was now in the enormous library downstairs, sorting through a pile of old dusty books. He'd already changed into his landlover clothes, a pair of jeans and a regular navy blue T-shirt. He was so beautiful, the way his gold-streaked hair hung to his jawline, the way the muscled contours of his chest and arms stretched his soft shirt. The broad shoulders and tall framework of his body screamed with raw masculinity.

Above all, though, it was his heart and sense of loyalty she loved the most. *And fucking Crazy Dirt is using those against him.* She loved him too much to let this happen.

"There you are." He beamed at her. "I think I've got everything I need. The pilots said the safety check is done. Ready to go?"

"Roen! Roen..." Liv's words faded as despair overcame her and she choked on her heartache. *"Please,"* she whispered, hoping with all her heart that he would come to his senses. *"Please listen to your gut, Roen." Oh God. I love you. Please don't go. Please.* Liv had no doubt in her mind that this...this *thing* intended to feed on their children someday, too.

Liv watched in horror as Roen and Crazy Dirt boarded the plane. Dana stayed behind, wanting to help Lyle, Dr. Fuller, and Holden with the task of transforming all of the women back.

Liv could do nothing as the love of her life flew away. With each mile of distance, the connection between her and her body faded—almost as if she wasn't strong enough to bridge so much space between them—until her body became nothing more than a flitter of tingles.

Liv immediately felt the isolation closing in on her, her soul anchored to the island, but one small connection remained: Dana.

CHAPTER SEVENTEEN

Five Weeks Later...

Roen stood in his corner office on the twentieth floor of Doran Cargo, gazing out the window across the Seattle skyline. It was so damned ironic.

Five months ago, he'd been standing in this very same spot, looking out this very same window, feeling a dark cloud hanging over his head. Then the envelope containing his father's will had showed up, telling him about the island. It all started from there, like a wild dream. He ended up taking a freighter out to the middle of the North Pacific, getting into a helicopter, and crashing into that island. He remembered seeing a vision of his mother trying to wave him back, telling him not to come to that place. But he had. And through a twist of fate, his mate had been shipwrecked and stranded there, too, forcing him to step in and fight for her. He ended up the leader of that strange place and found out who he truly was.

Yet for everything he'd been through, he still had just as many questions as when the journey started. He'd never got to the bottom of what the island was or what she truly wanted.

His phone rang on his desk behind him, and he walked over to check the caller ID. *Cherie.*

"Yes?" he said.

"Sir, your brother is on the phone. Should I put him through?"

"Yes."

"Oh! And Liv called five times. She said that if you don't call her back in the next hour, you're going to regret it."

Foking hell. He'd sent her to stay with her parents for a few days, taking advantage of the fact he needed to go to Chicago and sort through some legal matters with Phil. He'd been planning on leaving right after work. The truth was, however, that he needed a little time apart from Liv, too.

He ran his hands through his hair. "Thank you, Cherie. I'll call her in a minute. Put Lyle through."

"Yes, sir." Cherie stayed on the line instead of connecting him. She'd been doing that a lot lately, just sitting there listening to him breathe.

"Cherie?"

"Yes?" she said sweetly.

She was invaluable to him, but unless he did something to break her obsession, he'd have to fire her. That wasn't what he wanted.

"Cherie, do you trust me?"

"Yes, sir. Implicitly."

"Good. Then what I'm about to say may hurt

your feelings, but you need to trust me when I say that I don't want you. I will never want you—not in a romantic way. Not like I want Liv. Whom I plan to marry."

"You're going to marry her?" Cherie sounded heartbroken.

"Yes." He'd been planning to ask Liv right away, but then it didn't feel right. He wanted their memories to be free from the horrors of the last few months. In twenty years, they deserved to be able to look back at their engagement with fondness. Yes, it was best to put a little distance between them and that island, not just geographically, but mentally.

"So are we clear, Cherie?" he said in his absolute, most sympathetic voice. "Your obsessing ends today or you're going to have to find another position." He honestly did not want that, but if she didn't find a way to get control of her desire, it would ruin her life. And for what? She didn't love him. Human women just found his kind irresistible.

"Oh-oh-oh-kay, sir. I understand."

He drew a deep breath.

"Can you set me up with your brother?" she asked sheepishly.

What the foke? "No. Now please put the call through."

"Yes, sir. Here's your call, sir," she said, sounding more depressed than ever.

"Roen?" Lyle's deep familiar voice came through the speaker.

"Yes, I'm here. And please don't tell me you're calling with bad news."

"That depends," Lyle said.

"Depends on what?"

"If you see the fact I fucked Liv's sister as a problem."

Roen nearly choked on his tongue. "What did you go and do that for?"

"She's a woman. I'm a merman."

"You didn't…bite her, did you?"

"I'm not a complete asshole. And I have better control than that."

Most mermen didn't. Which was why in the past, women were only brought to the island during the Collection. The women would be bitten and some would become maids. Only now, he understood that women who drank the water were safe from whatever substance was in their saliva that changed the women into creatures.

Frankly, their species was very mysterious. One of the many reasons he wanted the scientific studies to continue.

"Well, I'm glad you didn't turn her sister into a maid, but Liv will not be happy regardless." Honestly, if he were Lyle, he'd be looking for another island to go live on. A change of identity would be wise, too. Ever since that final day on the island, Liv had been behaving strangely. She had an extremely short fuse and had become exaggeratedly controlling, suffocating. At first, he attributed it to the stress and exhaustion—after all, she'd been kidnapped by Shane and then had to kill in order to survive. However, five weeks had passed and he'd only seen her grow more frustrated. She was obsessed with getting pregnant.

Yes, he wanted children, too, but they'd been through so much. He wanted time together, just the two of them. Nevertheless, he'd agreed to just let things happen. He wanted her to be happy. She deserved that.

Only, she isn't happy. She's...foking crazy.

"Well, just a word of advice, brother," Roen said, "the Stratton women are a little...domineering."

"I actually find Dana rather—what's the term? Laid back. Except in bed, which is why I'm calling."

Roen resisted groaning. "Please do not tell me you're calling for sex advice."

"You wish, Roen. I need no help in that department. I'm a mermen."

"Then?" Roen parked his fist on his hip. He didn't have time for beating around the bush.

"Dana behaves unusually in her sleep."

Roen really could not give less of a foke. "Then don't sleep with her."

"You're not following; she gets hysterical and screams at the top of her lungs. She claws at my face and hits me."

Jesus. Lyle definitely needed to sleep alone. Or with someone else.

He continued, "She says that she's trapped, over and over again. That *you* have to be warned."

"Me?" Roen's heart skipped a dark, dreadful beat. "Foke. When did this begin? Why didn't you tell me sooner?"

"Hell, I only started fucking her a few days ago, after the barbeque."

They'd had a barbeque? If not for the very serious nature of this conversation, he'd be asking for details.

He continued, "And I'm still not sure she's not simply having nightmares."

"Does Dana remember anything?" Roen asked.

"Not a thing."

This was strange behavior, but it could be like he said: simply a nightmare.

"Do you think it means anything?" Lyle asked.

"I'm not sure." Honestly, he found it hard to make sense of.

"Has Liv been acting like herself?"

"No," Roen admitted. "I mean—I'm not sure. She's gone through a lot." He didn't have enough history with her to know if this was normal.

Bullshit. You've seen Liv at her worst. Even when her life had been threatened and she'd been locked in a cage on the island, there was a kindness in her. Yes, she was also a fighter and tough as nails, but her good heart always shined through. The same could be said about her selflessness.

However, since that last day on the island, she'd been behaving as though her heart had grown cold and distant. *Foke.* That thought hit him hard. "I have to go, brother."

"What are you going to do?"

"I'm not sure yet, but I need to go see Liv," Roen said, wondering if this had something to do with why Liv had been behaving so aggressively. "Lyle, have you sensed that anything is off at the island?"

"Actually, yes. I mean no. I can't describe it, but the place has changed."

"Changed how?"

"All of the maids have been turned back—well, most of them. Some remain as maids, despite being given water. Dr. Fuller thinks they simply gave up or let go of their human side. But the rest are starting to heal and remember who they were. The men are happy. There's a sense of hope and...well, it sounds fucking corny and ridiculous, but the darkness that once shrouded the place is gone. I'm beginning to think that was what made us so violent and bloodthirsty. But now, even the flowers are growing."

That did sound strange.

Lyle went on, "And when I say flowers, I mean they're everywhere, Roen. The island has turned into a paradise. Warm, beautiful, and filled with so much—" he made a deep little groan, as if seriously regretting what he was about to say "—love. The island feels like it's filled with love."

"You're foking scaring me, Lyle." This man, his "little" brother, was this fierce-looking, barbarian type, covered in scars and with a scowl that could stop a man's heart with one look. But to hear him speaking like some love-infatuated hippy, high on life and fresh ocean air...well, it was disturbing, frankly.

So Liv was acting like a raging bitch. The island had transformed into a happy little paradise. *Something is definitely wrong.* The only issue was, everyone had what they wanted. He had Liv. His people had peace and freedom. The human threat was gone.

"I'll be in touch." Roen ended the call and stared at the old book on his desk. It was their most ancient text, written in symbols similar to those found in the Phoenician alphabet, which made it difficult to read. The curious part was that all of their ancient texts had been translated over a hundred years ago into multiple languages. All but this one. It was why he'd taken it with him. Had someone simply destroyed the translated text? Or had this one been left untouched for a reason? Regardless, he had Cherie scan the entire thing and send it off to a linguistics expert in Germany. The stories in these old books were so outlandish—tales of mermaids and ancient fishermen, stories of an island that spoke—no one would ever believe a word of them. Ancient fairytales and nothing more.

He slid his cell from his pocket to call Liv.

She picked up immediately. "Where the hell have you been, merman?"

Roen cleared his throat. "Working. How are your parents?"

"Lame. They keep asking me about Dana. I mean, what more do they want? They spoke to her. She's alive. I'm alive. But my mother won't stop talking and talking and crying. I wonder how anyone puts up with her."

"I thought you loved your mother."

"Of course I do. I just find her annoying. That's normal, right?" Liv said.

"I wouldn't know. My relationship with my mother wasn't exactly normal."

"I suppose you're right. After all, she tried to eat you," Liv said callously.

"Thank you for the warm reminder." He still wasn't sure if the maid in the tank had been his mother, but what could he do now other than pray that whoever she was, she was in a better place? And truthfully, he'd spent almost twenty years grieving for his mother's death. And then he'd grieved for Lyle. He was done grieving.

"You're welcome, baby," Liv said. "Anyway, speaking of baby, I have some good news. I'm pregnant!"

Roen's stomach twisted into a knot. *Foke.* If something wasn't right with Liv, then her being pregnant would only complicate matters.

Then again, maybe this was why she'd been acting so erratic?

"Roen? You there?"

"Uh, yeah. I'm just..." he swallowed, "surprised."

There was a long moment of silence. "So, you're not happy?"

"Very happy. I think it just needs to settle in." *I'm going to be sick.*

"I figured you might feel that way, which is why I decided to come back to Seattle."

"But I told you, I'm leaving for Chicago. Urgent business." Now more than ever, he needed time to clear his head.

The doors of his office burst open, and in walked

Liv speaking into a cell phone. "Cancel it. We have some celebrating to do."

He lowered the phone from his ear and watched Liv saunter up to his desk with a victory swagger. She had her hair up in a clumsy ponytail, and her clothes were strange now that he thought about it, like she didn't know how to dress herself.

"What?" she glared at him.

He gave her a look. "I'm simply admiring your festive attire." Pink floral skirt with army green plaid T-shirt and flip-flops. Again, he found himself wondering if this was how Liv always dressed. He and she hadn't spent much time together in the real world.

"No. You're worried again," she said, giving him a warm smile. "I can see it in your eyes."

He set his phone down on his desk. "I've just been told I'm going to be a father."

Was she even telling the truth?

She walked around the desk, stood on her tiptoes, and gave him a kiss. Her lips were cool, but now he was beginning to wonder, was it really because he'd been running hotter? Why would he feel hotter? He'd had the island's water before. He didn't recall Liv's kisses feeling anything other than warm and wonderful.

All right. He had enough to suspect something wasn't what it seemed. The question was, what was he going to do about it?

CHAPTER EIGHTEEN

Liv did not know how much longer she could hang on or continue trying to break through. She spent each night screaming at Dana, just hoping her sister might hear. It had worked, but not on a conscious level.

And now her sister was sleeping with Lyle? Dear Lord, Dana really knew how to pick 'em.

He's way better than Shane, she thought, arguing with herself. *And way better looking, too*. But Lyle was…well, he was fucking huge. His muscles were like those big wrestler dudes on TV who spent eight hours a day beefing up. The first time she'd seen him, she'd almost wet herself. No. Not in a good way.

Yet, obviously he wasn't as vicious and cruel as he appeared. Or maybe he used to be and had changed? Because anyone who ruled this island of mermen—as Lyle once had—didn't gain control by being nice.

Although, things had definitely changed since

Crazy Dirt's departure. There was a new sense of calm and peacefulness that hadn't existed before. And in the early mornings, when everyone slept— except for the mermen who patrolled the beaches or the few remaining maids who came ashore in search of animal meat—Liv could hear the faint sound of her own heart. Somehow, it kept on beating, despite the fact that it was broken. But every pump was filled with hope for Roen, that he would somehow fix this and free her.

Where is he now? she wondered. Hong Kong? Shanghai? Maybe he was in his luxury penthouse overlooking Seattle. She tried to imagine him happy and safe, even if the woman he was with was a strange, evil creature from hell. And an imposter.

Liv imagined Roen gazing into her eyes and noticing that the soul looking back wasn't Liv's. *It's not going to happen. Fucking Crazy Dirt is too sneaky.* Which was why Liv felt her will to continue hoping diminish with each passing day. *And then your heart's going to give out.*

She remembered reading a study in her human psych class about how optimism, the sheer act of believing in a positive outcome, reduced the likelihood of heart disease by double-digit percentages. Hope mattered. It was like a vitamin for the soul. Hope was how she'd once survived ten days on a life raft in open waters. It was how she'd lasted five days without water under the intense heat of the day. She remembered thinking how her hope to see her family kept her going, until she realized there would be no rescue. That was the day she gave up. That was when her body began giving out. That was also the day she met Roen and her life changed.

It was kind of ironic, wasn't it? Had she given up sooner, she never would've met the island. But then she never would've gotten to meet that tall, fearless, sexy, stubborn man who melted her heart, melted her everything. Just when she thought life couldn't be worse and she had been at the end of her rope, the most wonderful, beautiful thing of her life had been waiting for her on the other side: Roen.

She sighed. She just needed to find the strength to carry on. She just had to believe that the most wonderful, beautiful thing in her life would be waiting at the end of this nightmare, too.

Keep hoping all you like, Liv. Crazy Dirt won. She got everything she wanted. And even if Roen figured out something was wrong, what could he possibly do about it? He couldn't get her heart back. It was gone forever, absorbed by this place.

And now, I'm the island. My absolute worst nightmare.

Roen knew that this was not going to be easy and could backfire on him. But he simply lacked a better plan and needed to know if something truly was wrong with Liv. If there wasn't, then he would beg her forgiveness. If there was, he wouldn't know what to do, but he'd cross that bridge later.

He sat at his desk, signing a stack of legal papers

Phil had sent to confirm Roen's temporary authority over his holdings. His mind spun in dizzying circles. A few weeks ago, he'd just assumed he'd leave everything in Liv's name. After all, they would be married soon and the assets would belong to them both. Of course, he hadn't asked her to marry him yet, and now he wasn't certain if he would.

He signed the pages with the sticky arrows and slipped out his phone to call Liv. He'd sent her home—to his penthouse—and told her they'd meet there after he finished some work.

The phone rang a few times before she picked up. "I hope you're almost home. I've been waiting here for hours," she whined.

Roen's heart sank for what he was about to do. "Actually, I'm hungry, and you're not much of a cook. Think you can be ready in forty minutes?"

"I cannot argue. Cooking isn't one of my finer qualities. But going out sounds wonderful—we can celebrate the news."

"I'll send my driver to get you. We'll go to the place around the corner from my office." It was a five-star steak house three blocks away. It was just the sort of place he would take Liv if they were really going to be celebrating.

"See you there, merman."

"Are you stupid?" he growled. "Do not call me that anymore. Someone might overhear you, woman."

There was a long moment of silence at the other end of the line.

"Did something happen after I left?" she finally asked with restrained agitation in her voice.

"Yes. We can discuss it over dinner. Wear something presentable, please. You dress like a child." He hung up the phone and blew out a breath.

That felt so wrong. The irony was that not too long ago, he had no issue behaving like a colossal prick with women. Or with men. He didn't give a shit about anyone but himself or his money.

He grabbed his briefcase and the suitcase he'd packed this morning and then called Cherie to send his driver to get Liv.

"You want the driver to get Liv and take her to the restaurant, but you're going to the airport?" Cherie questioned. "Is she meeting a friend there? Because I should change the reservation name."

"No. Leave the reservation in my name. And you are not to answer any phone calls from Liv. Are we clear?"

"Uh...yes, sir."

"Great. Call me a cab and tell my pilots I'm on the way." Roen's gut was already trying to tell him something. Something not-good. It was that he'd been too quick to believe that the nightmare was over. Who could blame him? After everything he'd been through, it was a normal reaction. But he should've known better.

An hour later, his plane was already up in the air, heading to Chicago. His phone rang, and he mentally prepared before answering. "Yes?"

"Roen, it's Liv. Where are you?" She sounded extremely upset.

"On my way to Chicago."

"Excuse me? But I'm here at the restaurant, waiting for you."

"Something important came up. I'll be home tomorrow," he said coldly.

"Are you joking?" she hissed into the phone. "We spoke an hour ago. We made plans. And couldn't you have at least called to tell me there was an issue?"

"Liv, I suggest you learn your place in this relationship. You are a woman, and I do not answer to you. I do not call and explain. I do not ask your permission. Your job is to look pretty and make me happy, which you've failed at. I suggest you get your ass home and think long and hard about your tone with me. You also might want to consider doing some exercise since fat asses don't get my dick hard. We clear?"

Roen held his breath, waiting for Liv's response. If there was one thing he knew about the woman he loved: She did not take shit from anyone. Not him. Not a deadly, psycho merman, and not a crazy island.

"Why this sudden change in attitude?" she asked calmly.

"You're pregnant. The courting phase of this relationship is over. Now we're moving on to the phase where you stay out of my hair and take care of my children. Why is this a surprise to you? It's how my people have done things for thousands of years."

Liv did not respond.

"I asked you a question, woman," he barked.

"I understand," she said, clearly pissed as hell, but refraining from telling him to go to hell, which was exactly what his Liv would do.

CHAPTER NINETEEN

"It's not Liv," Roen said to Lyle over the cell phone, still a few hours out of Chicago.

"Are you sure?"

"If it is, there's something very wrong with her."

"Or," Lyle offered, "perhaps the island is holding something over her."

No. Now that he'd started to think about all of the small inconsistencies—the way she dressed, her callousness with her family, her lack of kindness—and the fact her body felt cooler, he suspected the issue was far greater than the island's usual blackmail schemes.

"There's one other complication," Roen added. "She says she's pregnant."

"Fuck."

It was just one more red flag he should've seen but had not wanted to. Liv was all heart. She cared deeply about those she loved, and he had to believe that she would not jump so quickly and carelessly into motherhood. She would want to give their relationship proper attention before bringing a child in. She'd want to make sure she and he were ready. That didn't mean that Liv had never had the urge to go at it. Like him, she found her mate irresistible. But her obsession with getting pregnant so quickly should've been a red flag.

No, but you're an egocentric bastard and just thought your mate was so into you that she couldn't wait to have a little Roen running around.

All right. He wouldn't lie. He liked the idea of being a father—it fit well with his need to protect others.

Idiot. You've been played.

"Foke is right," Roen agreed, rubbing his forehead with one hand.

"She could be lying about the pregnancy," Lyle pointed out. "If the island is involved, that would be my bet."

"No, she probably isn't. Goddammit!" he barked at himself. *Why was I so naïve? A foking idiot.* "I should've known the island wouldn't give up so easily."

"I think you should bring her back here," Lyle said, "while we try to figure out what's going on."

Roen sipped his scotch and glanced out the small window of the plane, thinking about what to do next. Not that he gave a crap about his money, but he needed to speak with Phil about how to work around this. "Liv" couldn't be left in charge of the lives at his company. "I'm going to continue on to Chicago to meet with Phil. I'll have the pilots fuel up, and then I'll head straight to the island. I'll be there at first light, but I'm coming alone." He needed to learn what he could first before deciding what to do. *Still so many questions. Never enough answers.* "And Lyle?"

"Please don't get fucking sentimental on me. Because that sounds like where you're going."

"You and I don't do sentimental. Remember? We're mermen," Roen replied.

"True."

"I wanted to ask you something, and do not dare respond with a snide comment. If anything happens to me, Lyle, and for some reason Liv really is pregnant, promise you'll take if from her the moment it's born. Promise that you'll—"

"Roen, I can't—"

"You foking promise me, Lyle. You take that baby. You run. You do whatever you have to, but promise me it will be free from her. She plans to hurt it, use it, kill it, whatever… But no child of mine will suffer at the hands of that sadistic, psycho bitch."

There was a moment of pause. "I will do everything in my power to protect your child. If there is one. But for the record, brother, I'd like to say that you are a Doran. You come from an ancient line of the toughest men known to creation. Your name is the definition of strength among our people. I believe if anyone on this earth can conquer this demon, you can. You were born to remove this curse that's plagued us for thousands of years."

Roen took in his brother's words, wanting them to fuel his resolve to finish this nightmare hanging over their heads. But the truth was, fighting an enemy like this—one they never understood, shrouded in mystery—felt nearly impossible.

"Thank you, Lyle. See you in the morning." Roen ended the call, his mind furiously attempting to make the pieces fit.

The phone in his hand vibrated, signaling a text had just come in. He held it up and read: *Your urgent translation is done. In your email.*

The text was from Cherie.

Roen opened his email with his phone and stared at the tiny screen. His eyes skimmed. One page. Two. Three and four.

"Holy foke."

It sounded like a Grimm fairytale written by the devil himself.

☙◦❧

Sons of the Sea:

I write this story in hopes that one day my mermen brothers will read it and learn from my errors. For I have undoubtedly cursed our people for eternity and unleashed evil upon us all, upon our children, and upon their children. I know not what can be done to correct such a grave mistake, so I pour my knowledge onto these pages in hopes that the gods will guide it into the right hands.

It began when a wooden vessel carrying a large group of men—all with hair and beards the color of flames and skin the color of snow—spotted one of our women in the ocean among a school of dolphins. Our group often followed these creatures because their ability to sense sharks and other dangers was far superior to our own. We, on the other hand, are skilled at killing such predators. Hands are useful tools and our long tails give us speed.

I recall looking over my shoulder at the worried face of my mate, Salla. We'd been fleeing from these hunters for over a week, unable to eat, sleep, or rest. The men had the advantage in their numbers and their ability to rotate men to sail the ship. We both knew the humans were getting closer despite our efforts to lose them in a storm that had rolled in. The waves and vicious winds blowing against us made it difficult to swim any faster.

Soon the men would capture us in a net and take our tails, believing them to be magic and the means to everlasting life.

"Keep swimming, Salla!" I yelled, hoping that the violent winds, which inhibited our speed, would also slow down the humans who chased us, if not deter them altogether.

Fortunately, the turbulent waters had separated us from our group, and the connection we shared in our blood and hearts told us they were safely ahead. A blessing, I'd thought, because Salla and I were now the only ones being pursued.

However, as we swam, holding hands and moving toward an island up ahead, where we hoped to lose the hunters in the shallow waters filled with sharp volcanic rocks, a giant surge of seawater caught us both. It pulled us down so deep that our eardrums screamed. Just as I thought our bodies would surely give way from the pressure, a force of nature spit us out. Our bodies rose and rose until we not only reached the ocean's surface again, but we rode a cresting wave high above it. The wave carried us over land and then crashed with such force that I blacked out.

When I awoke face down in the mud, I panicked. Salla was no longer grasping my hand. I lifted my body and looked around, finding only dense forest.

"Salla!" I yelled.

But my screams were unnecessary. For when I glanced up at the form standing above me, I realized it was her. With legs.

"What happened to you?" I stammered.

Salla looked down at her body. "I-I do not know."

"You have legs."

She nodded in astonishment. "Indeed, I do. You as well."

I looked down at the length of my body and realized she spoke the truth. I too had humanlike legs.

"How is this possible?" I wondered aloud.

"I do not know, my merman. However, we should seek shelter. The hunters might be on this island."

I agreed with my female and proceeded to stand. The awkward feeling was exhilarating. Legs. I had legs. I could propel my body over rough terrain— rocks, hills, and even climb trees if I so desired. But how? How could this be?

"Do you recall anything, Salla, of how we came to be like this?"

"We were in a small lagoon with bright glowing water. You crawled out, but I was far too weak to follow. Then I felt my body burning with fire, and I realized I could walk out. As soon as I made my way to you, the transformation had taken place in your body as well."

The water was magic. Salla had once been a human, but it was unheard of to change back after being claimed. I, too, remembered having legs as a child, before the ocean called to me. "It is a gift from the gods." I felt tired no more. I felt strong and my mind felt sharp.

Salla kissed my lips and smiled. "The gods are looking out for us, my love."

By the time the sound of approaching footsteps caught my attention, it was too late. The human man had come from behind and pressed a knife to Salla's back.

It was one of the men from the ship, who'd been hunting us. The barren look in his blue eyes told me he was without a soul or heart.

"What do you want?" I said, but the man did not speak our language. He yelled and screamed, pushing the knife into Salla's skin, causing her to yelp.

Whatever the man desired, I could not fathom; however, I knew this would not end well.

I lunged at Salla and knocked her from his grasp. I pushed her away and told her to run as I moved to block the man from getting near her. The man came at me with his blade, but he was human, weaker and slower. I grabbed his wrist, turned his weapon toward his throat, and slit it. I paused only for a moment as I watched the blood pour from his wounds into the mud. He then mumbled words I did not understand, though I imagined he cursed me. To death. To suffer.

I ran in the direction where Salla had disappeared. She'd run through a stand of large pointed trees toward the center of the island, where a great mountain stood. How did I know this? A trail of blood.

My thoughts filled with panic as I ran as fast as I could with my new clumsy legs, wondering how the man had managed to cut her so badly. It was my fault. I had not been quick enough to free her.

I found Salla face down inside a giant cave that had more of that glowing green water. It illuminated the space with odd-looking lights that danced off the wet stone walls.

"No! No, no, no…" I turned Salla over and found a look of pain in her eyes.

"It hurts, Ari. It hurts." She held her hands over her wound, begging me to make it stop. Her cries were torture to my soul. There was nothing I could do for her. Nothing. The hole was too deep.

I took her to the pool and told her I loved her. The moment she understood what I meant to do, she began to fight and claw and scream. I held her under, knowing that this death for her would be far more merciful than bleeding to death from a painful wound to the stomach.

It shattered every part of my soul to end her suffering. I felt my heart fill with rage and anguish. I did not want to lose her. I screamed and wailed as she fought. Finally, her body ceased moving.

Broken, I pulled myself from the pool and dragged Salla out. That was when I realized her wound had healed.

The water was magic. Yet it had not occurred to me that it could repair flesh and bone.

I'd killed Salla. She could've lived if not for me.

I cried for many hours, mourning her loss, before I decided my life was no longer worth living. I decided to return to the hunter and get his blade.

"Ari? Ari? Where are you?"

"Salla?" I stood and turned, trying to see her with my eyes. But Salla's body still lay on the floor of the cave.

"Ari? I cannot feel my body. What happened? Why did you hurt me?" I felt her angry soul in the air all around me.

"I tried to help you. I could not let you suffer."

"You took my life. You, my mate." She sobbed with such agony, I was lost for words. My attempt to release her from her pain had only made her suffer more.

What had I done?

The next few hours I stayed in that cave, once again praying to our gods for help. I watched her body grow colder and colder. I could feel her anger and pain all around me. She had died at my hands and could not understand why.

"I think I can hear the others," Salla said. "I feel

them near. They are looking for us."

Salla still felt the connection to our tribe, just as I still felt the connection to her in my aching heart. "I will go find them."

"No! You cannot leave me. The humans will return. They will hurt me. I can feel two of those men getting closer. Oh, gods…" She began to sob. "They are going to kill me."

That was the moment I understood Salla's soul was trapped somewhere between this world and her nightmares and pain. "I will find the others quickly and return to you."

"They will make you leave this place. They will want to run from the humans, too." Her voice was frantic.

"I will not leave. I promise." I planned to find the humans and kill them. Then I would find our tribe and elders and discuss what to do.

"None of you will leave, Ari. None of you will leave."

"Salla—"

"No! I can see into your heart. You cannot leave me here all alone."

I had no intention of leaving her, but as much as I pleaded, she would not listen.

"I will kill them all, Ari. I will cook your brothers right in the ocean if anyone tries to leave." To prove her point, she made the ground shake and the water in the pool began to glow brighter, bubbling with heat.

I now understood that the magic in the water had only transformed Salla into something greater. I had no doubt she would harm our people.

When I eventually found our group on the other side of the island, Salla forced me to tell them lies so they would not leave. I told them how the island had spoken to me, that it was sacred and the creator of life in the world—a god that needed our help and protection. I showed them how the water was magic and gave us back our legs and made us stronger.

I hoped that over time, we would find a way to leave this place. But as I sit here looking out across the ocean, my body growing weaker and older, my last breath drawing closer, I know Salla will never release her hold on us, even though so few remain. Many have died attempting to flee. But Salla knows everything. She uses her connection with us to go inside our hearts. She whispers her evil thoughts into our souls. She says she will never let me go. Even in the afterlife I question if she will release my spirit or if I, too, will become a part of this place, where Salla's pain and rage touches every leaf, every rock, and every tree.

Those who remain without legs have lost their beautiful colors, their magic gone, their skin unable to stand the sunlight. Those who had children have now lost them, all killed by Salla as punishment for our disobedience.

Soon this record is all that will be left of our people. We have decided to stop eating, stop drinking the healing water that gave us legs, to embrace death rather than live as captives on this island.

May the gods have mercy on our souls.

❧

Roen scratched his short beard, trying to take in the astonishing yet tragic story. "Foking hell," he whispered.

He knew from the other texts and folklore what happened next in the history of his people, or what was believed, anyway. Afraid to be left alone, the island eventually compromised with their people, promising them freedom. Someday.

But so much of their folklore was shrouded in lies meant to keep their people from leaving.

Nevertheless, the story was amazing. The island and whatever supernatural properties it held were there long before Salla and Ari ever arrived. At least, that was what it seemed from the story. Of course, it was all told through the eyes of a merman who'd lived thousands of years ago. But could the island simply be some sort of natural anomaly, one that absorbed the sorts of energies that simply could not be seen with the naked eye?

Roen's thoughts stirred inside his head. If Liv really were speaking through Dana, it meant…well, she wasn't dead. She was trapped on that island.

But if Liv was trapped there, then who was inside her body?

Salla…

CHAPTER TWENTY

Sometime early in the morning, Liv felt a familiar energy approaching the island, but it wasn't until she picked up the vibrations in the air that she realized who it was.

Roen. He's coming back. Was Crazy Dirt with him? Liv didn't sense the malevolent presence.

And when the airplane landed and Roen took his first step on the soil, she could practically taste him—his strength, his love, his passionate soul. Her entire being swooned with joy. She only wished she had the ability to speak to him. Her guess was that Crazy Dirt had had many, many centuries to practice the skill of getting inside people's heads. Liv could barely get Dana to listen while Dana was asleep.

Roen then met with Lyle and a few of the other mermen. She could feel his soul was uneasy.

Can't say I fucking blame you. So many bad things had happened to him here. But then something unexpected occurred. Roen walked into the Great Hall alone, lay down on the floor, and began speaking to her. "Liv, I know you're here. Talk to me. Tell me what's happened."

"Roen?"

"Holy foke. I knew it."

❦

The moment the airplane doors opened, Roen knew Liv was here. "What the foke happened to this place?" he mumbled to himself, unable to believe that this was the same island.

Lyle and Dana were waiting for him at the end of the long dirt runway. The grins on their suntanned faces resembled those of a happy couple on a honeymoon. *All right. Now I've seen everything.*

Roen's eyes took in the surroundings. Exotic flowers of yellows, purples, and reds bloomed in patches mixed with green grass. This looked just like the dream he'd had.

This can't be.

The trees were again healthy, and he could hear birds chirping away. He looked up at the vivid blue sky and drew a breath of sweet, warm ocean air.

The scent of Liv was everywhere.

He looked at Lyle and Dana, unable to form words.

"It's quite a shock, isn't it?" Lyle said. Even Lyle looked like he'd had new life breathed into him.

"I can't foking believe it. And do you smell that?" Roen asked Dana.

"Smell what?" Dana said.

"That sweetness. It smells like Liv," he replied.

"I don't smell anything, but it has changed a lot since you left," Dana said.

"I don't think it has anything to do with me." It was the evil soul who hitchhiked inside Liv's body to get off of the island.

"I need a moment alone," Roen said. "I'll be in the Great Hall."

"We'll be in your house," Lyle said. "When you're ready, there is much to discuss."

Roen gave a nod and watched the two of them head into the forest, holding hands. He never dreamed he'd see his brother displaying affection to a woman.

He shook his head and made his way to the enormous cavern inside the mountain. Half of his heart prayed he was wrong about Liv being trapped here, and the other half prayed he was right. If Liv's spirit was trapped in this place, he wouldn't know how to free her. And if she wasn't here, then all would be lost. That woman who looked like Liv, possibly carrying his child, may have killed the love of his life.

He entered the Great Hall and couldn't believe his eyes. White light reflected from the water that sheeted down the walls and flowed into the pool toward the back of the giant cavern. The energy almost felt like a drug. Euphoric. The room even smelled like fragrant lilacs.

He lay down on his back over the shockingly warm stone floor and took a breath, trying to relax and take it all in. He felt the energy swirling all around him. She was here. He could feel her.

Roen then took a deep breath and opened his heart. "Liv, I know you're here. Talk to me. Tell me what's happened."

"Roen?"

"Holy foke. I knew it." Her voice echoed inside his head, and he jumped up off the floor.

"Oh my God, Roen. You found me. I can't believe you found me." The sound of Liv's joyful sobs saturated his heart.

He spent the next hour talking to Liv, pacing circles inside the cavern. She told him everything about the deal she'd made with the island to save them all. She told him how "Crazy Dirt" tore out Liv's heart and how Liv became anchored to the island.

He then told her about the text he'd read and how a violent tragedy took Salla's life.

"So the island is Salla. It explains why she's so crazy and paranoid," Liv said. *"Her story is like one of those movies about those poltergeists whose souls stay trapped in their violent deaths."*

"Only this isn't a horror film. This is real," Roen pointed out.

"Still just as scary," Liv said. *"What am I going to do, Roen? I can't stay here like this forever, and I can't go steal someone else's body. I'm not like her."*

"We need to set her soul free. We need to push her out of your body."

"But then what, Roen? My heart is...well...it's

part of this place now. And I don't know how to do what she did and just make one or pull myself out of here or whatever."

He had not told Liv the other part of the latest chapter, but he knew he had to. "Liv? There's something else I need to share with you."

"Oh boy. From the tone of your voice, I'm biting my nails. If I had nails. Which I don't. This is so damned awful."

"She's pregnant. Or your body is pregnant."

"What?" she barked. "No. No, no, no. She can't do that."

"I think she has."

"Why the hell did you fuck her, Roen?" Liv yelled.

"I'm sorry, but we both know I thought I was sleeping with you."

"Jesus Christ. She'll kill our baby."

"We don't know that, Liv."

"Oh. So you think she's going to be a loving mother who takes care of the baby after she almost wiped out your kind and killed all of the children as revenge when the first lucky settlers tried to leave?"

"No."

"She's probably going to suck the soul right out of the tiny thing or tear out its heart and get inside it."

"Who knows what she plans to do."

"Roen, this has to end. After the baby is born, you have to kill her. You have to end her."

"If I destroy your body, we lose all hope of getting you back, and what's not to say that her soul won't come right back here. As for the baby, if she truly is pregnant, then I fear what her evil soul is doing to it. I think we need to act now."

"I wish I could get closer and feel her. Then I might know what's going on. But she's too far away. She's just a faint noise like anybody else."

"You feel others?"

"I feel everyone, Roen. It's like a low vibration in the air. But I feel the ocean, I feel the trees and the birds and fish. It's really goddamned freaky."

So the island truly was connected to the rest of the world. He wondered about the other stories of the island being the spark of life.

"Can you communicate with anyone?" Roen asked.

"No. I'm not like Salla. I haven't had the time to practice being a giant asshole like she has. But I think it explains how she was able to get to me and Dana when we were back in Wrangell. Or why those pirates and Dr. Fuller dreamed of this place. I think it takes a lot of energy to reach out like that, but I'm sure it can be done if you have enough practice. And a giant stick of vengeance up your ass."

Roen laughed. Even now, in the face of such a colossal cluster foke, Liv was still Liv. "If it makes you feel any better, she's really bad in bed. I was beginning to dread having sex. Like sleeping with a cold fish."

"Whoa. Stop right there, merman. I don't want to know."

"Understood." But he felt guilty as hell.

A few long moments of silence passed, and then he heard Liv sigh.

"Liv, you need to know that no matter what happens, I will never abandon you. I will stay here with you until my last breath."

"You're not saying that because you're afraid I'll turn all psycho-Salla, are you?"

He smiled. "No. I'm saying it because you need to know that my heart belongs to you. No matter what."

"Thank you, Roen. But if there's a baby, it can't grow up here. It needs to be somewhere happy and beautiful. This shithole is no home for a child."

"I might have agreed with you three weeks ago, but now…"

"What? No. You are leaving here. You should set up camp somewhere else with the rest of your people. When they decide to leave."

Did she not know? "I think they'd be opposed to that, Liv. The island is changed."

"Changed how?"

He told her all about the flowers and the trees. He told her how good it felt to be here. *"I think it's you, Liv."*

"If only I had hands, I'd so be writing up my doctoral dissertation on this place. But, Roen, the reality is that Salla said she chose me because I was the only one strong enough to pull this off. But I think she's wrong, Roen. I feel like every day that passes I feel weaker and more hopeless. It's only a question of time before I end up like Salla. Batshit crazy."

"Then we will have to find a way to fix this, Liv." Though he had no clue how.

"The only thing you need to worry about is protecting that baby and killing that fucking bitch. That's it."

"We lose nothing by trying, Liv."

"Yes. We do. If she suspects anything, she'll use that baby as leverage against you. That is what she does, Roen. She uses those we love against us. She always has, and she always will. It's probably the only reason she wanted a baby in the first place. She's always five hundred steps ahead and she had to know you'd catch on sooner or later."

Liv had a point. "I am going to gather everyone together to discuss what to do."

"You can discuss all you like, Roen, but this decision is mine. And I'm not afraid to die. Especially if it will end Salla once and for all. Let the baby be born far away from this place and destroy my body. With luck, she'll be too far away to come back here."

That was taking a huge risk on a huge assumption, and not that he didn't understand Liv's point, but she couldn't understand what it would do to him if she died. And growing up without a mother...well, he wanted better for his child. They had to try to undo this.

"We have to attempt to bring you back, Liv. We have to try to release Salla's soul. Please. If not for me, then for that baby. Our baby."

Liv remained silent for several long moments. *"Okay. We'll try."*

Roen wanted so badly to hold her in his arms and kiss her. He loved her brave heart. He loved how selfless and strong she was. How could he have been fooled by that bitch parading around in Liv's skin?

Liv was special and she was strong. And like her, he would not go down without a fight.

CHAPTER TWENTY-ONE

Liv listened to the voices bouncing around inside the Great Hall. Roen, Lyle, Dana, Holden, Dr. Fuller, Amelia, everyone was there. Even the mermen who were once loyal to Shane now ranted with anger over what had been done to Liv.

And then there were those whom she'd never met. She couldn't count them all, but there had to be well over a thousand women, some standing inside the cavern and just outside, every one of them vowing to do whatever it took to save Liv.

It was very touching.

"We will not let history repeat," said Jason, who was one of the men who'd thrown her to the maids to be eaten alive. Of course, he had been under orders and mermen were notoriously loyal, so she didn't exactly hold a grudge. "I owe you and Liv everything, Roen. You gave me back Amelia. You freed us. I can't..."

I don't believe it. Is mister tough-guy merman crying?

Liv listened to a crack in his voice followed by the distinct sound of a hiccup. *Ohmygod. Why can't I see this?*

"Roen, please tell me someone is videotaping this just in case I get my body back, because I really want to see a merman cry."

"Hey. Do not make fun of me," Jason grumbled.

"You can hear me?" Liv asked.

"Yes. I can." Even he sounded surprised.

"Anyone else?" Liv asked.

An ocean of voices responded.

"But how? Why now?" Liv wondered aloud.

"I think," Roen said, his voice deeper and louder than all of the others, "if you open yourselves to Liv, you'll be able to hear her."

"Liv? Oh shit. Liv! Are you okay?" Dana said.

"I'm here, honey. I'm fine." Liv felt the connection growing stronger.

It's amazing. For years, she'd hypothesized that the bond between people wasn't simply mental or emotional. There was something real that connected one person to another—mothers and children, soul mates, siblings, best friends—however, people today simply lacked the science to measure it. But her thesis paper had focused on this very thing. She'd even gone as far as creating experiments to measure brain waves of a person when someone who loved them thought about them. It proved that the connection between people far exceeded the sentimental realm. Love's reach went beyond what anyone could see or sense.

She glowed with a sense of deep, humbling

emotion. She couldn't see, but she could feel the connection with these people who loved her. Of course, the connection with Roen and Dana felt stronger.

"If I had a body right now, I'd be passing out hugs. Thank you, everyone. Can I ask a question here?" Liv wondered aloud. *"I read some of the old translated text. One of them said that your people once had the power to control the air and water around them. It said that mermen and mermaids were once beautiful and magical. If this place draws from the energy of everyone, would it—I mean, wouldn't I be more powerful if...well, you know?"*

"You mean that we should stop drinking the water," Roen said.

"It suppresses the fish gene—or whatever," Dana pointed out.

"We are not fish, woman," chimed in one of the men.

"What I think Dana is trying to say is that in our human forms," Roen said, "we are weaker because we are not in our natural state. If we were to return, we could be more powerful."

Liv could feel everyone connecting the dots, just as she had. If they were all connected and she and this place could literally draw their energy, wouldn't she be more powerful if they were more powerful? *"I might be able to push Salla out if I were strong enough."*

"We owe everything to you and Roen," said Lyle. "I will stop drinking the water."

"No. You should stay here by my side," Roen argued. "I may need you if something should happen to me."

"I think we should all stop drinking the water," Holden said. "Everyone except for Lyle. Hell, who knows? Maybe we'll like being fish again."

Multiple people booed him. They hated being called fish.

"Then it's decided," Roen announced. "We are going to stop drinking the water immediately and give Liv everything we can so that she can send Salla straight to hell. Or wherever the foke evil souls of our kind go."

"*Roen...*" Liv said. *"I didn't mean we'd do this today. We have to wait until after the baby is born."*

"So she'll have a chance to kill it? No. We do this as soon as possible."

"My body has no heart, Roen."

"You will do exactly as Salla has done."

Meaning she'd do what? Make a heart out of water and push it into her body?

"I don't know how," Liv said.

"Liv, let me ask you this: do you believe that Salla has good intentions for our child? Do you believe that she wouldn't kill it in a heartbeat to serve her own purpose?"

"No. And no."

"Then we must take this risk. If you fail to push Salla out, I do not believe she'd give up your body or destroy it—she's wanted her freedom for far too long."

Roen had a point. If Liv failed, little would

change. And she agreed that Salla would not give up her body or change course. They lost nothing by trying.

Liv wanted to draw a sobering breath, but that was what people did—people who had lungs.

"*Promise me,*" Liv said, "*if anything goes wrong, if it looks like she's going to threaten the baby, that you'll all back down.*"

No one spoke up and Liv could feel the anxiety spike.

"*There's been enough dying,*" Liv said, "*and now we all know the truth about this place, about her...it's only a question of time before we end Salla. Let's not do that at the sacrifice of one more innocent soul.*"

CHAPTER TWENTY-TWO

Later that evening after the meeting concluded, Roen called Salla and set the wheels in motion. He had only his faith in his love for Liv and the ruthless instincts he'd cultivated in his human life to guide him through this.

"What? You're at the island?" Salla barked over the phone.

"I am not well," Roen explained.

"Oh. When did this start?" she said innocently.

"I think the moment I left the island. I don't know for sure, but I passed out, and when I woke, I asked the pilots to fly me here."

"Did you drink the sacred water?" she asked.

"Yes. But—" he coughed for effect "—it only gave me temporary relief. I thought if I came back here, I might heal. I don't know what that foking island did to me." Roen didn't want her to suspect that he'd caught on. He had to convince her that he was still blinded by the body and face of Liv.

"How are you feeling now?" she asked.

"I won't lie; I feel the same."

"I'm coming there."

"No," he protested. "There's nothing you can do and the island is not safe for you. Now that you're carrying our child, you must stay away from this place."

"Roen—"

"Listen to me, Liv. You heard how I spoke to you before. I treated you like shit, and I didn't care. Something is happening to me. Something bad. You must stay away."

He heard a loud sigh. "If you are not well, I must be at your side."

It was exactly as Roen hoped, but they weren't quite ready for her yet.

"I cannot prevent you from coming," he said, "but I ask you to do what's right for our child." Of course, she didn't give a shit about the child, and she would try to get on a plane to the island as soon as possible. Unfortunately for her, there were only three corporate jets. One was on the island. The other two were in for repairs—a manufactured coincidence, of course. "I'll call you later, but I have to go now."

"Okay," she said solemnly.

Now all that was left to do was focus everything they had on Liv. If anyone could finally put an end to Salla, it was her. The love of his life with a heart big enough to fuel an entire island with hope.

꩜

Three days later…

"She's on her way," said Lyle.

"What? Now? We need another day. Or perhaps even two." Roen set his book down on the coffee table in front of the fireplace. He'd been reading to Liv, listening to music with her, and spending every moment he could laughing and sharing memories. The good ones, anyway. There had been so little time for the two of them to simply talk and know one another. Liv, for example, told him that when she was growing up, she and her two sisters had dressed up as mermaids for several Halloweens. "It was fate you became my mate, then," he'd said. He'd told her how when he was little his best memory was of his mother's smile. Things had never been easy for him and Lyle growing up, but her warm eyes and reassuring smile never failed to comfort him.

Meanwhile, life around them on the island had slowly begun to change. He and Lyle were the only ones taking water. The rest of the men—nearly two hundred total—had all decided to endure the painful change back to their natural state. Even some of the women asked to be bitten, but Liv wouldn't hear of it. She said they'd all suffered enough.

So now it was up to the mermen to make this happen. What everyone wondered, given how the island had changed, was if they would become those creatures with the yellow glowing eyes or turn into the creature of their legends. No one knew.

"She got tired of waiting. She chartered a plane," Lyle explained.

"Foke. That gives us five hours at most," Roen said.

"I think we should rethink this, Roen. We're not ready," Liv chimed in.

"I think we need to check in with Dr. Fuller first." She'd been monitoring everyone and documenting their transformations. Like before, each man was growing weak and black spots appeared on his skin. And as of this morning, about half looked like they were about to die—shallow breathing, weak pulse, coma-like state. "If we need more time, we'll have to figure something out."

"You can always take her to bed," Lyle suggested.

Roen shot him a look.

"What?" He shrugged. "It will keep her busy for a few minutes."

"Very foking funny, brother. Can you be serious for a moment?" Roen grumbled.

"I am being serious. Pretend to be excited to see her. Spend the next few days keeping her in your room."

Roen hung his head. "I can't. There's no way my cock will get hard for her."

"You're a foking merman. You've faced greater challenges."

"He's right, Roen," Liv chimed in. *"You have to buy us more time. No one's transformed yet."*

Foking bloody hell.

"*Just pretend it's me,*" Liv pushed.

That was impossible. His imagination wasn't a superpower. "I will try to play the role of passionate mate and attempt to distract her. But if it doesn't work, be ready to move forward, Liv. Do what you can."

"*Just remember. You promised me that you'd back down if she threatens our baby.*"

"I will. I promise," Roen said.

"*Okay, then tell everyone it's time for radio silence. They can't hear me. I can't hear them. Salla can't know that we're all so strongly connected now, and she certainly can't know that you and I have been talking. Complete radio silence.*"

Everyone had already discussed this point before they initiated the plan. Hopefully no one would slip up. Salla would arrive, see the island in a new state—that couldn't be helped—and Roen would whisk her away to bed while everyone else finished transforming. Once Dr. Fuller gave the green light, Liv would begin pulling strength from them and push Salla out. To where? No one knew. But the souls of the dead went somewhere. Liv simply had to break Salla's bond to this place.

"*Just one last thing, Roen: I love you.*"

"I love you, too, Liv."

"*I'm afraid,*" she said.

As was he, but the one thing he'd come to learn from all of this was that one couldn't give up hoping and trying. If you failed, you just dusted yourself off and kept going. How many times had he almost died these past few months? How many times had they faced the impossible? Honestly, he'd lost count. But as long as life kept giving him chances, he'd keep taking them.

"The mermen have a saying, Liv. There is a time to eat. There is a time to fuck. And there is a time to kill."

"Jeez. How inspirational. I'm feeling the tingles of victory already."

"The point is, Liv, there is nothing else. It doesn't say a time to feel sorry for yourself or give up. It doesn't say there is a time for fear or even a time to die. Because those aren't options. There is only living and fighting. That's it."

Liv sighed.

"So what time is it?"

"Time to kill," she said reluctantly.

"Try it with a little more conviction, woman." Roen laughed.

"I'll never make a good merman."

"There's a reason Salla chose you; you're strong. Stronger than she is. You just don't know it yet. And with us helping you, you'll be even stronger. Now, can I get another one? What time is it?"

"Oh, stop being so corny. I think I liked you better when you were a complete hard-ass."

"What's that? I couldn't hear you. Did you say you like my hard ass?"

Liv laughed. *"No, I said—"*

"Because I cannot blame you. It is mighty and strong like a manly oak. Or is my ass more like two halves of a boulder? I don't know."

Her laughter died down. *"I love you, Roen.*

Whatever happens, just know that I'm glad I got to meet you—it's been one hell of a ride."

"The ride's not over yet, my love. It's just getting started."

But as that plane grew closer, even he could feel Salla's cold presence growing stronger. *There's no time for doubt, man. That's not on the list of options either.*

CHAPTER TWENTY-THREE

Roen felt Liv's spirit all around him. It was the one thing giving him comfort in this very critical moment.

Salla was only a few minutes away, and according to Dr. Fuller, no one had completed the transformation.

"It can't be long now," Dr. Fuller said, looking up at Roen with her deep, worry-filled brown eyes, holding a stethoscope over Holden's heart. "His body is fighting, but he's barely got a pulse."

"I think you need to lock yourself in a room upstairs—just to be safe," Roen said.

"Why would I do that? Someone's got to stay and document what happens," Dr. Fuller argued.

Stubborn landlover. They were always so damned curious. Funny, he sort of liked it. It reminded him of Liv. Nevertheless… "If they turn into those voracious creatures, you'll be nothing but a meal to them."

"I'm not leaving Holden."

Roen looked at her, beginning to understand the situation. "You like him."

"He's a doctor. I'm a doctor. We have a lot in common, including our fascination with this island. And he's still single." She shrugged.

"Okay. Well…good luck to you, then. I hope he doesn't bite your head off. Literally."

"I'll take that risk. Good luck with Salla," she said.

"Thank you. Where's Dana?"

"She's doing the rounds with Lyle, checking on everyone and reporting back in to me."

Holden groaned, and Dr. Fuller leaned down and kissed his forehead. For a moment, Roen could see the spark of love in her eyes.

Of course, mermen were irresistible to human women. That said, he could see that perhaps her feelings were more than lust. Given how long Holden had been alone, mateless, he could see him being happy with a smart woman like Dr. Fuller.

"You two would have beautiful children together." Holden was your typical-looking Irish, pale skin, bright green eyes, curly, long flaming red hair. Dr. Fuller was a lean, athletic beautiful black woman with short curly hair.

She gave Roen a strange look. "Do I look crazy to you? I'm not marrying a fish."

Roen glared at her, and she cracked a smile.

"Ha. Funny," Roen said.

"I'm sorry, you know. I'm sorry for all of the trouble I caused everyone."

"It wasn't your fault," Roen replied. "You were a pawn—no different than any of us. And now, you're going to help us usher in a new era."

"We could heal a lot of people with the water here," she said.

Generations from now, this island might be the key to stopping much larger problems on the planet. And there wasn't enough water here to save every sick person in the world. "Tell the public about this place—the instant healing effects of the water—and every government in the world will be fighting to get their hands on it. The powerful and greedy will destroy this island. We must protect this place, study it, learn from it. With that knowledge, we can do more than simply help a few people."

She blinked at him and smiled. "I guess you're right."

He dipped his head. "Now all we need is a little luck. Be careful, Dr. Fuller. Once he changes, he'll be hungry."

She winked at him. "Oh. I hope so."

Oh-foking-kay.

೨৽৽৻

Roen stood at the end of the landing strip, feeling like he was about to go on stage in front of an audience of thousands. Yes, it was something he did well, like any CEO who had to give speeches in front of one hundred and fifty thousand employees or investors all around the world. Being under pressure was where he excelled.

This situation, however, was an audience of just one, but everything was on the line. *Breathe slowly. Calm. Confident. You are foking Roen Doran.*

The plane's doors flew open and the small staircase extended out. Salla emerged looking like she'd put some effort into dressing more like a grown-up—a snug T-shirt and jeans. She'd left her hair down today.

Showtime. He pasted on a smile, but did not go to her. He had to act as though he wasn't feeling well, as he'd told her on the phone.

Holding a small travel bag, Salla made her way to him, the expression on her face as she looked around displaying her shock.

"What has happened to this island?" she asked.

He shrugged and then reached for her shoulders as soon as she was close enough. He bent his head and kissed her passionately, trying his best not to think about how cold she felt.

He pulled back and beamed into her eyes. "I don't know what's happened. No one does. But I've missed you, Liv." He pecked her lips. "I'm going to take you back to the house and show you just how much."

She gave him a curious look. "I thought you were sick."

He offered his most winning smile. "Oh, but I am. Which is why I must return to bed immediately."

"I'm serious, Roen."

"So am I." He sighed. "I continue to feel weak, but we can discuss that later. First, I need to get my cock inside you and make up for how I treated you."

She smiled at him. It wasn't real.

Now he could see it so clearly—every blink of her eyes, every smile that twitched across her lips, all fake.

His cock was about as hard as cooked spaghetti.

"Let's get you back to the house, then," she said.

He placed his arm over her shoulder, noticing the coolness of her body.

"How are you feeling, Liv?" he asked.

"Great. I mean, it's odd to feel another heartbeat inside me, but it's what I've always wanted."

"You can feel the heart?" Roen's stomach flipped.

"Yes. Of course I can. It's your baby. He's strong. He'll be the strongest merman yet."

He suspected that was what she wanted: Stronger mermen so she could use them just as she'd done for thousands of years. Once they showed any signs of weakness, they'd miraculously end up dead— challenged to a fight by another merman or simply killed for breaking a law. There had always been someone dying on this island for "legitimate" reasons that really just served to cull the herd. It was also why she ensured there was a steady stream of new mermen on the way, and she carefully chose which women came to the island and became pregnant.

Genetic engineering at its finest. If by chance one of the women turned out to be a man's mate, she got to serve in another capacity—as a maid and protector of the island. She would also serve as leverage to keep her man in line. Life on this island had been a well-thought-out system meant to serve Salla's needs.

Well, that's all going to end. Fucking bitch.

"Roen, you're shaking," Salla said.

Foke. He really was. But it was from anger, not from illness. "The walk made me tired. I'll drink some water and lie down. I'll be fine." They made their way up the long steps that led up to his home.

"I can't get over how different this place feels," she said. "Why didn't you mention it?"

He tried to play it casual. "I don't know. It didn't seem as important as seeing you. What took you so long to get here, anyway?"

"The jets were under repair."

"I would've sent the one we have here back for you," he lied.

"You told me not to come; otherwise, I would've asked."

"I was a fool to think I could be separated from you for very long, Liv. I've been going crazy not seeing you."

"It was the strangest thing," she said suspiciously. "The mechanic working on the other two jets kept telling me the parts were on the way and they'd have the repair done, but then the parts didn't show and then it was the wrong part."

"I'll have to speak to him about that." He pushed open the front door, moving as slowly as possible. All for show, of course.

"Don't worry about it. I fired him and then had

your little bitch Cherie charter a plane. Oh, and I fired her, too."

"Why did you do that?" He tried not to sound upset. He really valued Cherie.

Salla shrugged. "I don't like the way she talks about you. And because I can. I still own your company."

Roen bit back his anger. "She can't help obsessing. After all, human women find me irresistible." He winked at her and they made their way upstairs to the bedroom.

The moment they entered, he felt a sense of dread overwhelm him. Could Salla sense it?

He stopped next to the bed and sighed dramatically.

"What is it, Roen?" she asked. As if she gave a shit about him.

"I think that hike wore me out. I'm not sure I can...you know." He gave her a look.

She smiled. "No problem. You rest for a while. I'll come back later."

"Where are you going?" He couldn't let her leave.

"To explore. I want to see what's going on with this place. It's so quiet. Too quiet. Haven't you noticed?"

"Not really."

She turned to go.

"Wait! I've missed you. Let me have a drink and we can take a shower. Perhaps you can help me along?" He lifted his brows suggestively.

He seriously doubted it, but he had to try. He

needed to buy more time to allow Liv to be ready to fight Salla.

"You don't look like you're—"

"You're denying my request?" he said, lowering his voice, deciding to play hardball.

"No, I just…"

"Then take off your clothes and get your sexy ass in that shower."

Salla gave him an irritated look.

"Please?" he added, in a not-so-nice tone.

She huffed. "Fine." She kicked off her tennis shoes, pulled her T-shirt over her head and then slid down her jeans. She then removed her undergarments and strutted naked into the bathroom.

Her body was still Liv's—beautiful, soft, womanly curves; sweet, full breasts; and a nice round ass. She'd even put on weight, which he loved. She'd been far too thin when they'd first met, a result of her having been stranded at sea for ten days without food.

She turned on the water, and he tried to just focus on his favorite parts of her body—the parts that aroused him: her pink nipples, the patch of dark hair between her legs, those lips. He loved her eyes most, but he couldn't look at those. Liv wasn't inside.

Roen stripped off his suede and looked down at his cock. It now stood straight up, long and proud, the tip bright pink and just begging for what was between those legs of hers.

"Well, well," Salla said. "Looks like someone is

feeling a little better."

He gripped his cock in his hand. "Little?"

"Okay...hugely better." Standing under the steaming spray of water, she beckoned him with her index finger. "Now get in here and fuck me."

He stepped inside the shower and pressed his lips to hers, grabbing her thighs to part her legs and lift her. Pushing her against the wall, he maneuvered his cock to her entrance and thrust inside her.

Cold. She's so cold. He just wanted to get this over with. *Don't foking think about it. Don't...*but he could already feel his cock going soft.

He pushed inside her again, wanting so badly for his body to obey and want this, but his heart simply couldn't be lied to. Not anymore.

This woman was not his mate. She was vile and a monster. She'd destroyed so many lives, including those of his parents. He and Lyle had also suffered.

Liv stopped kissing him, and he looked at her, about to make up some lame excuse for his lack of enthusiasm, but she spoke first. "When did you find out?"

He gave her a look. "Find out what?"

"Do not play games with me, merman." Salla's voice—the voice he'd learned to hate, the voice of the island—came through like a poison to his ears. "And do not *fuck* with me—remember that I've got your precious Liv's body and your baby."

He released her, and she slid down the length of his frame. He fought the urge to scrub his skin raw, while his mind quickly went to work. His experience with the island had taught him three things: one, she was cunning. Two, she was ruthless. And three, she was arrogant.

Okay, she still doesn't have a clue what we're planning or that I've spoken to Liv. The element of surprise was still on their side.

"What the foke did you do with her, Salla?"

There was a moment of shock in her eyes, followed by a wicked smile. "So you finally figured out who I am." She stepped around him out of the shower, making her way over to the towel rack with a cocky little strut. She didn't fear him. She didn't fear anyone.

Big mistake.

She went on, "I knew you would, merman." She began toweling off, and he stepped out of the shower, standing only a few feet away. "It's why I chose you, you know. You're smarter and stronger than the rest." She threw the towel at his chest, and he caught it. "And that Liv; you and her are like fire and gasoline. Together you generate such delicious energy. I knew you'd be perfect."

"What. Did. You. Do. With her?" He towered over her, doing his best to get her to continue talking. Every minute that passed was another minute closer to his people being transformed. Hell, if he got lucky, Miss Cocky Bitch here might even tell him what she really planned to do.

"She's here, Roen. Her heart so full of love and strength is fueling everything—but I'm guessing you already know that, too. Don't you?" She shot him a look, but he held is poker face.

"What do you want, Salla?"

She shrugged. "I've already got what I want. A powerful merman who'll give me powerful children. And, at least for now," she waved her hand in front of her body, "a body."

A little click went off inside Roen's head. That body wouldn't last forever. "You can't have daughters. We're only able to make male offspring." It was part of the way their species had evolved. Why? How? He could only guess, but the females always came from the human world. All it took was one bite from a merman and they transformed.

"Ah." She raised her finger. "But the stronger the merman, the stronger the mate they'll choose."

So she didn't plan to kill the baby, she planned to make more. Probably as many babies as that body would permit. And her hope was those sons would go off and find nice, healthy strong women who could serve as vessels.

"I gotta say, Salla, I'm impressed. But you do realize you need me to foke you for your plan to work."

She laughed. "Oh, you're so wrong, Roen. You see, I have come to realize that you were right. My ways were archaic. It's like…" she waved her hands through the air, "I'd been living in the dark ages and just waiting for my time to come. The age of technology has freed me."

He stared at her, waiting to hear the sadistic punchline.

She slipped on her panties and jeans and threw on her T-shirt. "I don't need you people anymore.

You took care of those vile humans with your new security team. As for that useless cock of yours…" she pointed to his extremely limp penis, "I just needed you to fill a cup."

He crossed his arms over his chest. "Good luck with that, because I won't be jerking off for you."

She laughed and cocked her head to one side. "Oh, honey. I've collected enough of your powerful merman sperm to last a lifetime."

He frowned. "When?"

She winked. "Oh now, do you really want the details of what I did with all that cum from your five daily ejaculations?"

Dear foking hell. No, he did not.

"The fertility clinic is wonderful at providing those little collection kits and accepts deposits twenty-four seven."

"You're one sick bitch, Salla."

She pointed at her skull. "I'm one smart bitch, merman. But I owe my transition into the twenty-first century all to you."

"All right. So you no longer need me or my people. What next?" Would she tell him?

No. She was too smart to tip her hand.

Suddenly she came at him with a knife.

He grabbed it and twisted it into her stomach. It was purely a knee-jerk, self-defense reaction.

"No!" he cried out the moment he felt the warm, wet liquid oozing from the hole he'd made right in her upper abdomen.

He dropped his hand and looked down. Salla did the same, a look of shock in her eyes.

"You…stabbed me."

He hadn't meant to. She'd come at him, and he'd grabbed her hand. Before he knew it, he'd twisted the blade around and had plunged it inside her.

"Foking hell, Salla. What did you do?"

Her mouth flapped as she looked up into his eyes. "You…you…stabbed your own mate? Why?"

He realized that she'd thought it impossible.

With tears in his eyes, he gripped her shoulders. "You are not my mate, Salla. You evil foking bitch." Because now she'd destroyed Liv's body, their baby, his everything.

Salla dropped to the floor, a vacant stare in her eyes.

"No. Godfokinghell. No."

"Roen?" Liv's sweet voice filled his head. *"Wha-what happened?"*

"She's dead," he whispered, falling to his knees, looking at the body in front of him.

"Who, Roen? Who's dead?" Liv's voice was filled with panic.

"Salla—I mean you. Your body."

"No. Oh God. No."

"I'm sorry," he sobbed. "She came at me with a knife and I just…"

"It's okay, Roen. It's okay. I know you didn't mean to."

The rage inside him was too much. "It doesn't foking matter what you believe; I killed you and our child." He could never live with that. "I destroyed any chance you had to come back."

"Roen…?" Liv's voice was choked. *"Bring my*

body to the pool. There's still a heartbeat."

Roen froze for a moment. He remembered the story in the ancient text. Ari had tried to bring Salla back. It worked, but it was unclear what had happened.

"I'm here, Roen," Liv said. *"Just come to me."*

His vision blurry with tears, he scooped up the body and made his way to the Great Hall. "I'm on my way." He simply prayed that whatever came back into this body, it would be Liv. And the other tiny life inside would be all right.

Liv could practically taste Roen's anguish. It was dark and bitter and filled with so much hate.

"Dana? You there?"

"Yes, Liv. Ohmygod. What happened?"

"Salla tried to kill Roen."

"And?" Dana asked.

"And she lost."

"Oh no. Oh no. What does that mean?"

"It means…I don't know."

"And Cray-Cray?" Dana asked, frantic.

"I don't know that either. I don't feel her presence anymore, but the body—my body—still has life in it. Roen's going to the Great Hall."

"We'll be right there, Liv."

"Whatever happens, Dana, tell Lyle that Roen can't self-destruct."

"I won't let him," Lyle responded.

Of course he'd been listening in. Everyone could hear her.

"Here he comes…" Liv said. *"Pray for us."*

Roen entered the Great Hall and didn't stop until he reached the pool. He jumped in with both feet forward, cradling Liv's body in his arms. He watched as the water covered the wounds and her torso.

"Please, please, please bring her back." *Bring them both back.*

With his eyes closed, he held her tight, wishing for the impossible.

After several minutes, he looked down and saw that the wound was the same.

"No," he cried, running his hand over her forehead. "It's not working."

Liv, after all, was resistant to the healing effects of the water. The very thing that made her strong also made her vulnerable.

Roen held her tight, feeling his heart gripped with despair.

"It's all right. There was nothing you could do," Liv said.

But there had been. He could've let Salla stab him. "Tell that to our baby."

"Roen?" Lyle spoke from somewhere behind him. "I'm sorry, brother. But where is Salla?"

He shook his head. "I don't know," he whispered.

How could this have happened? He'd lost his hope of a future with Liv and any hope at all.

"Roen, honey. Don't give up. I can feel them."

He wiped his eyes. "Who?"

"Them—the mermen. They're waking up."

CHAPTER TWENTY-FOUR

At first, Liv was unsure, but the blatant rejoicing in Dr. Fuller's voice was unmistakable. Then Liv felt them. At first one and then two. Then three and four. Ten and a hundred. The seconds sailed by, and she felt them all bursting to life.

Were they sea monsters? Were they something else? Liv only knew they were no longer the mermen she'd first encountered—violent, angry, coldhearted. And they were a hundred times more powerful than before.

She could hear their hearts thumping away like two hundred war drums beating in unison, surging with defiant rage. They savored their freedom and would do anything to crush anyone who tried to take away who and what they were.

In a million years, Liv couldn't begin to explain the swell of emotions she felt radiating from their collective soul, but she finally understood why Salla had never wanted to let them leave. The mermen were an ancient people who'd evolved, survived, loved and fought for each other and their mates. Their bond was unlike anything that had ever existed. Their power came from each other. Their strength came from each other.

And in this moment, they were fighting for Liv's soul.

Without a second thought, she began pushing every ounce of energy she could muster into her body, willing it to heal. Liv immediately felt something happening. Tingling and pulsing. Warmth and light. She felt herself moving into her body.

"Hi, you fucking cunt. Thanks for bringing back your body," groaned a familiar hate-filled voice. "I knew you could do it."

Salla. She wasn't gone. She was right there, her soul clinging to Liv's flesh and bones, like an evil hermit crab.

"I'm not letting you do this, Salla. It's time for you to go."

Salla laughed. "Who's going to make me?"

"We are." Liv's soul surged with a powerful, warm, white light. She wondered if that was what love looked like when everything else was stripped away. So pure, so euphoric and healing.

"What are you doing?" Salla growled. "Get the fuck off of me!"

Liv could see bits and pieces of what was happening through her own body and eyes. Roen was holding Salla down to prevent her from physically going anywhere.

"I love you, Liv," he said, grunting his words as

Salla flailed. "You can do this. You're stronger than she is."

Liv felt Salla's soul struggling, trying to hang on tightly to Liv's physical form. She could almost see Salla, too, though it was difficult to describe. Her energy was black with swirling bits of red—like part of her soul was just as angry as it was evil.

"This body will die if you do that, Liv," Salla screamed.

But Liv couldn't allow Salla to live a moment longer. These people had suffered long enough. She and Roen had suffered enough.

"I'm going to crush you, Salla. And if my body dies with you, so be it." There was no doubt in Liv's mind that given the chance, Salla wouldn't harm just her child, but thousands more for generations to come.

"Liv! Don't!" Roen said.

But as much as Liv wanted a life with Roen and to be a mother, Salla's world was filled with too much suffering. Now Liv could see everything, every memory, every life Salla had taken. As Liv tried to overpower Salla, she saw right into Salla's evil heart—how she seduced the mermen into this violent life, blinding the truth from them. They'd always had the power, and she'd always been afraid to be left alone, that the humans would hurt her. Salla's nightmare became theirs.

And this place? This place was what it was—an island in the North Pacific. Its bedrock made from crystals and minerals that created a kind of energy that couldn't be seen with the naked eye or measured with any instruments in this day and age. It truly was special. And all the life that blossomed around the island since Salla's departure? It was how the island was meant to be. A paradise.

"And you're nothing but an uninvited guest, Salla. And it's time for you to go."

Liv felt Salla shrinking under the weight of her conviction.

"You fucking bitch! I'll destroy you. I'll destroy your baby, your mate, your entire family!" Salla yelled aloud, but her words only fueled Liv's determination.

"I'm not afraid of you anymore, Salla. No one here is. You have no more power over me, them, or this place. So go to fucking hell!" Liv felt Salla dissolve into nothing. After several long moments, Liv knew that she had finally done the impossible.

"She's gone. The bitch is finally gone." A wave of utter euphoric happiness swept over her. *"Roen?"*

He was silent, but then choked out, "Your body…"

Oh no. Her body was dying. *"Place my body back into the water,"* Liv instructed. She didn't know what to do, but she wouldn't give up. Not now.

Too anxious to sit, Roen stared down at the beautiful sleeping form on the gurney in one of the recovery rooms inside Holden's home slash medical clinic. The machine to Liv's side quietly beeped.

"She's going to be fine," said Dr. Fuller, standing behind him.

Roen looked over his shoulder. "I didn't hear you come in."

Dr. Fuller leaned over Liv and checked the IV.

"Why hasn't she woken up yet?" Roen asked.

Liv had gone silent the moment he'd put her body back into the water. Then she began breathing again, and he'd wept with joy. Everyone had.

Only, she hadn't woken up, and he could no longer hear her speaking to him. Neither could Dana or Lyle.

"I don't know," Dr. Fuller said regretfully. "But she's only been out for a few hours. Give it time."

"How's the baby?" Roen asked.

Dr. Fuller gave him a look. "Fine. Just like the last time you asked ten minutes ago." Holden had an ultrasound machine—hell, they had everything on the island—and Dr. Fuller had used it to take a look. A tiny heartbeat had been present, which was a miracle in itself. And from the size of the baby, Dr. Fuller was sure it was about five weeks old. That was the time he'd been with Liv, the real Liv, so there was a chance that they'd conceived the first time. Regardless, that's what he would choose to believe.

Dana entered the small sterile-looking room with Lyle. The red eyes made it obvious she'd been crying.

"You're exhausted," Roen said. "Why don't you go lie down in one of the beds in the other room. I'll call you if anything happens."

Dana looked up at Roen with those big brown eyes that were so much like Liv's. Even Dana's heart-shaped face and lips were similar. "I just took a power nap. That's why I'm here. I saw Liv in my dreams. She was laughing and swimming in the water with all of these…" Dana leaned in, "mermaids."

"Mermaids?" Roen asked.

"You know, the ones with the pretty long hair and sparkling green and blue tails."

At first, Roen thought she was joking, but she wasn't.

"But she can't be swimming," he said. "She's right here."

Dana made a sad little shrug. "It was just a dream. But I had to come see her." She walked over and leaned toward Liv on the bed, planting a kiss on her forehead. "Come back, Liv. You're not a mermaid."

"Should we do some tests to see what's going on with her?" Roen asked Dr. Fuller.

"I'm hesitant to do more than blood work, since she's pregnant."

But doing nothing but waiting felt completely wrong. He had to take action. He had to do something to make her better.

Roen took a seat in the chair beside Liv and rested his head on her chest. Her heart thrummed away at a steady pace. Her breathing was calm and normal. He lifted his head and looked at her. "Where did you go, Liv?"

❧

Liv had felt her soul release from the island, but something powerful began pulling her away from her body, pushing her toward *them*. Some were the shapes of mermaids and mermen with magnificent bodies and long flowing tails. Some were simply lights that mingled and swam in the air, dancing around a fire.

I could stay here forever, she thought, feeling like she was in a beautiful dream.

"But you need to go back, Liv," said a soft female voice.

Liv looked up at the woman with long flowing hair and big eyes. There was no color to her, just light. Sparkling, beautiful light.

"Did I die?" Liv asked.

"No, sweetie. But you will if you don't return." The woman simply smiled at her. "You don't belong here. Not yet anyway."

"What is this place?" Liv asked.

"This is the island. The part that cannot be seen with eyes."

Liv didn't quite understand. "You mean all of the energy in that place…this is what it looks like?"

"Yes. Now that you've freed us all from Salla," the woman pointed behind Liv, "your life awaits you."

Somewhere in the back of her mind, Liv knew

she had to go. But her heart wanted to stay and be near this beautiful light. Whatever it was.

"I don't want to leave," Liv argued. "I like it here. I feel safe."

"Liv, Salla didn't choose you. We did. We tricked her into finding you and into thinking you were the one who could free her. But we chose you because you are strong and you have a pure heart. It was why the maids protected you, why Salla couldn't control you, and why my son fell in love with you."

"You're Roen's mother," Liv realized. *Roen. Roen...* An image of his hazel-and-green eyes flashed in her head. It was coming back to her now. The reason she wanted to go back. But then there was a problem.

"My body," Liv said, "I couldn't get inside." Yes, now it was all coming back to her.

"Your new heart wasn't ready, but it's done now. Your body is completely healed."

Liv covered her mouth. "I have a new heart?"

"A gift from all of us."

That is one hell of a gift. "Thank you, but how is that possible?"

"Never you mind that. Just tell my sons I love them. And that I'm grateful they set me free." The woman embraced Liv and then she felt herself falling and falling. The sound of beeping and a warm strong hand over hers flooded her senses. Cool, clean air filled her lungs and her body began to tingle.

Slowly, Liv opened her eyes and saw Roen, his

head resting on her chest, his eyes closed as if listening to a beautiful symphony.

"Roen?" she whispered.

His eyes flew open. "Liv?"

She made a little nod. "Yes, merman. I'm back."

He lifted his head, and his eyes began to tear up. "Thank God." He jerked forward and kissed her hard. He pulled back and grinned. "You're warm. So fucking warm."

"Yes, it's me. All me. No hitchhikers."

"But where were you?" he asked.

"I'm not really sure. I think I was here, but I wasn't here. And...I don't know." She blew out a breath. "And your mother says hi. She's so happy, Roen. And she loves you. You and Lyle. Yeah, and I think she said something about wanting to thank you for freeing her."

The waterworks really turned on and Roen began to sob.

She couldn't keep her own eyes from tearing up. "Okay. Stop that. I thought you mermen were supposed to be tough."

He wiped his eyes. "I'm going to punish you for that." He grinned, the tears still trickling from his eyes. "As soon as you're feeling up for it." He looked down at her body.

Then it struck her. "Ohmygod. The baby. Is it all right?"

He nodded. "Five weeks old and a heart like a lion. A mer-lion, of course."

Liv placed her hand over her stomach. Now it was her turn to sob.

"Oh, look who's the big baby now." He sniffled.

She smacked his arm and laughed. "Me. I am. And...I love you so much."

He leaned forward and kissed her. Her lips parted and his tongue slid between her teeth, stroking her gently, passionately and making her feel like she just might need to try out her new heart right then and there.

"Eh-hem." A deep voice came from the doorway.

They stopped kissing and looked at Lyle, who stood there grinning. "I see our fair queen has returned to us." He dipped his head. "But I knew you would."

"How?" she asked.

"This island is magic. Don't you remember? And we are forever grateful to you, Liv."

"We're in the middle of something here," Roen snapped playfully.

Lyle nodded. "Yes, well. I came to show Roen something very interesting, but now that you're awake, you must see it, too. Are you well enough to move?"

"What is it?" Roen asked. "You know I foking hate surprises, Lyle."

"Don't be such a pussy and come with me," Lyle pushed.

"I want to see," Liv said enthusiastically.

"No. You need to rest," Roen protested.

"I'm fine. I've never felt better."

"You're such a mother hen, brother," Lyle said, a teasing gleam in his eyes.

"Before I forget," Liv said, "your mother says hi, Lyle. And she wanted to thank you for setting her free."

Lyle's jaw dropped. "My mother was the woman I killed?"

Liv and Roen both nodded, and then Lyle proceeded to start crying like a giant, seven-foot baby.

Dana suddenly appeared next to him. "Lyle, what's wrong?"

Dana then looked at Liv and put her hand over her heart. "Oh shit. For a minute I thought he was crying because you'd died. But you're awake!" She rushed toward her sister, pushed Roen out of the way, and hugged her. "Oh, thank God," she cried.

Liv patted her sister on the back. "I missed you, too."

"You have no idea how scared I was, Liv." She pulled away and wiped her eyes. "I was afraid I'd have to tell Mom, Dad, and Krista that you really were dead this time." She smiled and then whooshed out a breath. "But now we get to have babies together."

Liv felt her smile melt away. "Babies?" Both she and Roen glanced at Lyle, who suddenly looked guilty as hell.

"I'll wait outside." Lyle quickly disappeared.

"Dana," Liv said, scolding her.

"What? I wanted a merman of my own. And now I got one."

"But he's a…"

"Eh-hem." Roen stood behind Dana with his arms crossed over his chest.

Liv looked at Dana and sighed. "Welcome to the family."

CHAPTER TWENTY-FIVE

Liv, Dana, Roen, Lyle, and Dr. Fuller stood on the boat dock, staring out at the horizon to the west. The sun was just setting, turning the sky a stunning shade of orange.

"What are we looking at?" Liv asked, the reflection of the sun dancing off the waves, making it difficult to see anything at all.

Lyle pointed to a spot in the water where something splashed around. "There! Look over there!"

Liv tried her best, but it just looked like a dolphin or something. Maybe even a shark.

"It could be anything, Lyle. What do you think we're looking at?" Roen asked.

Just then a figure jetted up from the water and then disappeared underneath the surface. It happened so fast, Liv wasn't at all sure what she'd seen. But it looked like… "Was that a shimmering blue mermaid?" She looked at Lyle, who grinned and wiggled his brows.

She then looked at Roen, who just stood there staring as if he'd seen a unicorn.

"Well, I guess we know where our people went," Lyle said.

"So they're not coming back?" Dr. Fuller asked, seeming very disappointed.

"I have no idea," Lyle said. "But I think you should stay here indefinitely and take over studying the island."

Dr. Fuller stared at something off in the distance. It was a large hand waving at her in the water. A blue tail then popped up and began doing the same. Was it Holden?

"I think I'll go get my swimsuit." Dr. Fuller grinned and walked off.

Okay...

"Roen? Can I ask you something?" Liv whispered to Roen, trying to keep a straight face. "Do mermen have penises?"

"What?" He laughed.

"I've always wondered, you know, if they're half fish down there...is there a penis? Does it just dangle around?"

Roen shook his head, chuckling.

"Don't make fun of me. It's a legitimate question," Liv said quietly.

"Well, maybe I'll stop drinking water so you can find out." He cocked one beautiful, caramel brown eyebrow.

"I would totally do you as a merman. Especially if you had a sparkly tail."

He pulled her close to him, their mouths inches

away. "Let's just focus on regular sex for now. We can save the kinky stuff for later."

He kissed her hard, making her heart flutter. A heart that she'd freed from the island, but now belonged to Roen.

He broke the kiss and scooped her up into his arms.

"Ohh…are we going back to your place, merman?" Liv asked.

"I can't wait that long." He marched up the hill, away from the docks and through a stand of trees. The trail hooked around a bend and opened up at a large lagoon with a waterfall.

"I remember this place," she said as he laid her down on the grassy bank near the water's edge. This was the place where they'd once held the strange ritual to see which merman could hold his breath longer. It was all part of their elaborate claiming rituals.

"You know, Roen, you never really claimed me properly." She smiled at him.

"I'm not going to bite you, Liv. Not while you're pregnant anyway. But I do have other plans."

He pulled down her shorts and pushed up her T-shirt, exposing her breasts to the warm evening air.

He whipped off his shirt and then shed his own shorts. His long, thick erection jutted out and made her core throb with anticipation. She spread her legs for him as he knelt and looked down at her most intimate spot.

"Mmmm…" He stroked his hand over her gently. "You have no idea how sexy you are, Liv.

Every inch of your warm, warm womanly body."

"I kind of prefer my view. It's way hotter." Her eyes stuck on his pulsing cock.

He took it in his hand and leaned forward, teasing her entrance and c-spot with the soft, velvety head. She flung back her head, savoring the sinful sensation. She then arched her hips toward him, silently inviting him to give her more.

"You're so wet, Liv. So ready for me."

She looked up at him, those strong bulging biceps tanned to perfection, the hard contours of his pecs, the deep grooves of his rippling abs. *Exquisite*. That was what Roen Doran was. But what made her hotter than hell was the look in his eyes. Like he wanted to fuck her, bite her, eat her up.

"What are you waiting for?" She ached for him. She craved to feel his cock sliding deep inside and filling her body, pumping and grinding against her.

There was a moment of pause.

"What's wrong, Roen?"

He winced. "I really do have the urge to fucking bite you, Liv."

She propped herself up on her elbows. "Oh. And you think you won't be able to control yourself?"

He shook his head no. "That's not the problem."

"Then what?"

"I never wanted to bite her. Not once. I should've known, Liv."

He felt guilty. He needed her to say she forgave him.

She smiled at him and reached for his neck,

pulling him down on top of her, settling him between her thighs.

"Roen, I know you love me. And I don't feel bad about a thing. I won. And I won you." Not only that, she freed them both.

"I still want to bite you." He grinned.

"How about just a nibble, no skin breaking." She trusted him with her life, now more than ever.

He covered her mouth with his, his tongue working rhythmically against hers as his hand reached down between their naked bodies. He positioned himself at her entrance and then moved to grab her hands, raising them above her head and pressing them into the soft grass.

When he thrust his hard cock into her, she gasped with pleasure, breaking from their passionate kiss. She looked into his eyes and noticed how they seemed to shimmer with a million shades of green and flecks of golden sparkles. He moved into her again, holding her in place as he went deeper. She tried not to look away, but the sensual pleasure was too much.

"I think…" She panted. "I think I'm going to…" She was already too close.

"Uh-uh. Not yet." He withdrew and turned her over, raising her hips and putting her ass up in the air. "I'm not even close to being done with you, Liv."

He slammed into her from behind, his powerful arms holding her in place as he pistoned his hips. Her ears filled with the sounds of his deep, masculine throaty groans, the sounds of his skin slapping against her bare ass, and the rhythmic humming of her moans.

"Oh God, Roen. Don't fucking stop." She could never get enough of this. Of feeling his slick, hot cock sliding into her, pushing against that magical spot deep inside. He went on and on, not slowing down.

"I can go all night, Liv." He fucked his words into her. "But I won't."

He flipped her over and once again kneeled between her thighs, holding his thick, rock-hard shaft in his hands. He slid the head up and down over her c-spot. "You ready to come, Liv?"

She could barely speak. The erotic view of his glistening head massaging her swollen, throbbing bud was too much.

She gave him a quick nod and threw back her head, bracing for his hot, hard thrust. He gave it to her, driving himself all the way in. She exploded and came hard, screaming his name, grabbing fistfuls of dirt and grass, trying to keep herself from losing her mind.

Her screams only made him let go. She realized he'd been holding back, being gentle with her. But now he began fucking her harder, using his entire body to pound his cock into her.

She began climaxing again. "Harder, harder, Roen." She just wanted him deeper, just wanted more.

His body slapped and she opened her legs as wide as they could go, wanting more.

Finally, as the second wave of sinful contractions

racked her body, Roen pillared his hands on either side of her head and arched his back.

He groaned toward the sky, pouring his hot cum into her, his entire body shuddering with his dick twitching deep in her core. With short little thrusts, he finished emptying every drop inside her, finally collapsing onto his elbows.

The two lay there panting, their sweat-slicked bodies pressed tightly together, his hard flesh still inside her. After a few delicious moments of feeling their bodies floating down to earth together, he raised his head and began kissing her.

"That was amazing," she whispered in between sweet lazy kisses.

"I'm not done yet," he whispered back, and began moving with slow shallow strokes deep inside her. "I have a lot of bad memories to erase."

"But I don't think I can again." It was so, so good. Every muscle felt like a ball of quivering Jell-O.

He kissed her neck and bit down softly, coaxing a little gasp from her mouth and triggering tiny tingles on her c-spot.

"Just relax," he whispered against her neck, pulling out just a few inches and easing himself back in. "I'll do all the work."

She laid her head back and looked up at the night sky. The sun was completely gone now and there were millions of twinkling stars above them. She let out a breath and savored the feel of the hot man on top of her. "I love you, Roen."

"I love you, too. Now, open those legs a little

wider. I'm going to show you the real power of a merman."

EPILOGUE

Two Years Later...

Liv watched a seemingly endless parade of unbelievably beautiful, heavily tattooed men march back and forth in front of her. Every one of them was nearly seven feet tall, ripped from head to toe, and wearing nothing but shorts and snug-fitting tees practically bursting from the seams as they unloaded wooden crates from the small cruise ship's cargo hold.

"You better not be eyeing my men, wife," Roen's deep voice whispered from behind her.

Liv smiled. "Well...you know how partial I am to those fish-scale tatts. Gets me all excited." She turned and found Roen looking down at her, frowning. "I'm just joking," she said. "You know you're the only merman who gets me all wet." She snorted. "Get it. Wet? You're a merman and—"

He kissed her. "Silly human."

"But seriously, I think your men should all go back to the whole man-skirt thing. That was pretty hot."

"Liv, stop teasing me. You know how jealous my kind get—"

"Honey! Are we in the cottage on the left or the right?" Liv's mom's voice called out.

Liv tilted sideways and looked around Roen's large frame. "The white one on the right. It's bigger!"

"Okay, honey!" Liv's mom disappeared up the path toward the cluster of guest quarters that overlooked the harbor.

Liv brought her attention back to Roen. "Thank you for inviting my family to stay for a while." Even Krista had decided to come and help Dr. Fuller with the studies on the island. Krista, a veterinarian specializing in marine mammals and birds, would be in charge of documenting the wildlife. The non-mer kind.

Roen beamed at Liv. "I know how much your family means to you. And I have to say, your parents have adjusted really well to all of this."

They'd actually told her parents everything right before the baby had been born. Or make that babies since Dana had hers too. But days before their due dates, there'd been a moment of panic when Liv'd had a terrible dream that Salla had done something to the baby and it came out with a tail. The thought kind of freaked her the hell out, but she'd told herself she'd love the little mer-munchkin no matter what. But still, it made her think about all of the lying and how much damage had been done to her relationship with her parents. And even with Krista.

It was time to tell them everything.

But Liv would never forget the looks on her parents' faces when she told them the truth—being shipwrecked, getting kidnapped—twice—killing to save her own life—also twice. At first Liv was sure they were going to have her locked up, but then her father had said something that blew her mind. "The people in Wrangell have known about them for ages. There are legends going back generations, old fisherman songs and stories about how they once protected our island. These last few hundred years, they just ordered their supplies from us."

"Supplies?"

"Yeah. Boat parts, fishing supplies, food, satellite dishes—you name it. The businesses in town make a big part of their living from them."

Flabbergasted, Liv's mouth just sort of flapped for a while. "But...why...why didn't you say anything?"

"Did you not meet them?" her dad asked. "Those are some of the scariest, most ruthless assholes I've ever met. And when a seven-foot-tall, walking killing machine throws cash at you and says he'll kill you if you ever tell anyone, the merchants took it seriously. No one dared speak of them. Ever."

Liv couldn't believe it. All that time, her parents knew? And so did most of the small business owners on the island. But now that she'd thought about it, it made sense. There wasn't a whole lot of tourism on the island because it was so remote and only accessible by small plane or boat. The fishing industry was almost nothing. Yet, people seemed to live fairly well. Now she knew why.

Anyway, it took a while to convince her parents that things had changed and she and Dana were not insane for wanting to marry two giant "mean" mermen or have their children.

After the babies, Pike and Cruise, came and her mother saw Roen and Lyle being so gentle with their newborn sons (yes, sons—with legs. And lungs of steel and the screaming capability to match), all hesitations flew out the window. Pike, by the way, was the name she and Roen chose for their son. Yes, he was named after a fish—kind of an inside joke since Liv had been so worried that Pike would be born an actual fish. Pike also meant "spear," so Roen liked that his son's name signified something dangerous and deadly. "A real merman's name," he'd said. Dana chose "Cruise" because she said that being taken for the Collection and going on that cruise was what led her to Lyle.

Strange thing to want to remember, a cruise that brought her to an island where she almost died, but okay.

Anyway, Roen wanted a small quiet wedding, free from the paparazzi, who still stalked him every time he stepped on dry land. It got even worse after Phil filed for their marriage certificate. The world wanted to see the infamous billionaire bachelor marry the shipwreck-slash-kidnapping survivor Olivia Stratton. That made it impossible to book a church anywhere, so they ended up having the ceremony in Wrangell a few months after Pike was born.

As for Dana and Lyle, they were engaged, but Dana said she wasn't going to tie the knot until Lyle showed her his sparkly green tail. Which he refused to do. Of course, Dana was absolutely head over heels in love with Lyle, but Liv suspected the two didn't really care about getting a marriage certificate. They were both too busy having sex all the time and being new parents.

She and Roen, on the other hand, had billions of dollars in assets they needed to have jointly owned. First, for their son, and second for the island. They both worked like mad to have a private research center built right next to the Great Hall. It had just been completed, and Phil had successfully (and discreetly) hired seven of the world's top scientists in the field of physics, molecular biology, genetics, and environmental biology. Naturally, they would've preferred to use mermen, since most of them studied at some of the world's top universities, but most of the science geeks were not coming back. So, she and Roen decided they'd have to trust a few smart humans to do the work. This island was far too important not to take the risk of letting a few in on the secret. Not when they were both convinced that the island held the key to healing the planet someday. With so much pollution and global warming, the work they started today might be the only hope generations from now.

That was also why she and Roen had decided to move back. Liv had finally finished her PhD—yes, she was Dr. Olivia Stratton now—and the research center was complete.

Also, Dana and Lyle already lived here, as did Dr. Fuller and Holden, along with about one hundred mermen and five hundred mermaids. Some of them were couples who'd decided to come back and live as humans. Some were single. At least for now. The rest, however, had taken human form and returned to living as landlovers or stayed at sea. Liv had only seen the creatures a few times with her own eyes, but she'd seen plenty of the photographs taken by Dr. Fuller and Holden for their studies. The mermaids—even the ones who'd been unable to change back—looked exactly like the beautiful creatures from fairytales—happy, ethereal, and majestic with long flowing green or blue sparkling tails. The mermen, however, well...dear God, they were even bigger when in their natural state—larger muscles, broader shoulders, and yes...a very impressive dangly penis. Liv still wasn't sure about how all that mer-anatomy worked, but the thought of learning someday intrigued her.

If only I could get Roen to stop drinking that water for a few days.

"So are you ready to go unpack?" Roen asked, nuzzling her neck.

Liv turned in his arms. "You just want to have sex." Frankly, so did she. She could never get enough of Roen in bed.

"Yes."

"Well, Pike's with Cruise, taking a nap at Lyle and Dana's. I suppose we could go and do some unpacking over by the lagoon. Naked." She winked.

"I was thinking we might try for another." His greedy, greedy gaze stared at her breasts.

"You just like seeing me with big boobs."

"Yes." He smiled. "You know your breasts have always held a special place in my heart since the day we met."

She laughed and walked away from him.

"Where do you think you're going?" he griped.

"We can have another baby if you show me your tail."

"You just want to see what my mer-penis looks like!"

She kept on walking toward the house. "Yep!"

A deal's a deal, merman.

Concentrate, Salla. You are not weak. You are strong. Salla watched the tiny dinghy approaching the sandy beach. All she needed was for the man to get close enough. *That's right, you fucking bastard. Come to Salla.*

The tiny boat slid up onto the sandy bank, and the fisherman hopped out. She wasn't strong enough to see him, but she could feel him. His energy, his thoughts. And he was heading straight for her.

That's right. Just a few more steps...

"Hello there, big man."

The man stopped walking. "What the fuck?"

"Do not be afraid, my sweet strong man. My name is Salla. And if you come just a little closer, I can make all of your dreams come true…"

THE END…?

AUTHOR'S NOTE

All right. So I don't know if I'll make a habit of this, but some of you may have noticed how every book I write always has a hidden meaning— acceptance of self, letting go, embracing adventures, striving for the impossible, looking beyond appearances, being grateful even when life isn't perfect.

FUGLY was the first book I ever actually said anything about because the theme was so near and dear and raw to my heart. But your touching emails and messages made me think. Maybe no one cares about why I write a particular story, but maybe some do.

So if you're into hidden meanings, be sure to check out the breakdown I did for you at the end here.

For those who just want to know one thing: **"Mimi, got any swag?" The answer is yes!** I have a lovely pile of signed MERCILESS bookmarks with the evil Shane on them and I have thank you magnets ("I am a merman. What have *you* done for the world lately?") for those who mention that they posted a review. Just shoot your snail-mail address to mimi@mimijean.net

And KING FANS!!!! I'm now working on MACK for a February 2016 release. **PRE-ORDER for Kindle, iBooks, Kobo, and NOOK, here: http://www.mimijean.net/mack.html** Or sign up for my mailing list and I'll shoot you an alert once it's available.

HAPPY READING!
Mimi

2016 Release Schedule:

MACK (King "Trilogy" Book 4) February
TOMMASO (Immortal Matchmakers, Inc., Book 2) May
TAILORED FOR TROUBLE (Happy Pants Series) August

Note: GOD OF WINE (Immortal Matchmakers, Inc. Book 3) will release either May or October, depending on how well my boys behave. Haha…

THE MERMEN TRILOGY.

WHAT'S IT REALLY ABOUT?

While *Mermen* is an adventure about a young woman who faces some very difficult situations to survive and ultimately be with her true love, it's also about a man and a group of people who've been robbed of their humanity, hearts, and freedom. When I see the devastation happening to refugees around the world, families and lives destroyed by political agendas, I think of the island. There's no soul or love to be found. Just greed, darkness, and want. The oppressors often hide behind religion, but it's a mask. They don't care about God (in any form), they don't care about their people, the children they scar, or anything but their own power.

And the soldiers who fight on behalf of these "leaders" rarely start out as bad men. They get sucked in. Poverty and violence towards their mothers, fathers, sisters, brothers, wives, and children turn them into people who commit heinous atrocities to those who are weaker. They rape, murder, and torture in the name of their cause. If we look at the ones who start out on the peaceful side—the victims—then it's the victimizers' cruelty that will eventually change them.

Either way, it's a zero-sum game. What's left behind is a culture of hate that is so strong, so powerful, that generations from now, they'll still be fighting and killing. (Sound familiar?)

The mermen, obviously, aren't as cruel as some of the groups we see victimizing entire populations in the Middle East (not even close) or in other regions, but they do represent this particular breed of mindless obedience that allows a person to justify violence. "My god tells me to do this." "The island says we must." Fear is a big part of what drives this behavior.

So then, how do these people, who've endured so much (the soldiers and their victims), rise above the pain and oppression instead of fighting and suffering for the next hundred generations?

Love.

Hands down, it's the most powerful thing anybody can get, give, and feel. I believe it's more powerful than hate and fear, and it's why I write Romance.

Hell no! I'll never be an advocate of sitting idly by while men who've been corrupted with hate and fear rape women or little girls and kill mindlessly (as we're seeing in Syria, Africa, and in so many other war-torn places around the world), but when and where, if ever, will this stop? With the men who fight and are too gone to know any better? Not a chance.

Hope lies with us—the mothers, sisters, and daughters who have the ability to shape what our children think. Even if it's just a quiet whisper, telling our children to believe in something greater, to believe in love...It's the only path forward that I can see. Hate and killing equal more hate and killing.

The mermen were wrong when they said that life is only about eating, fucking, and killing. Liv showed them all that there's also a time to love and that it's far more powerful than anything else. Yeah, it's corny. But that's the breakdown of the story. Hope you enjoyed!

With Love,

Mimi

ACKNOWLEDGEMENTS

A huuuuge GARGLE-GARGLE-ARRRR… (maid speak for "thank you") to my MER-ciless peeps! I think I might have been certifiable for a few weeks there, but your encouragement and support were like sacred water to my poor writer brain. Thank you: Kylie Gilmore (oh, yeah—I made you read another bloody book!), Dali (run while you can!), Ally, Bridget, Latoya, Pauline, Su (awesome cover), Period Images (sa-weeet photo shoot!), and Stef @ writeintoprint.com!

Thank you to my dude-crew for many Peet's Coffee runs and for putting the toilet seat down every once in a while. Love you.

Mimi

MACK (FROM THE KING TRILOGY)

Coming February 2016
PRE-ORDER NOW! www.mimijean.net/mack.html

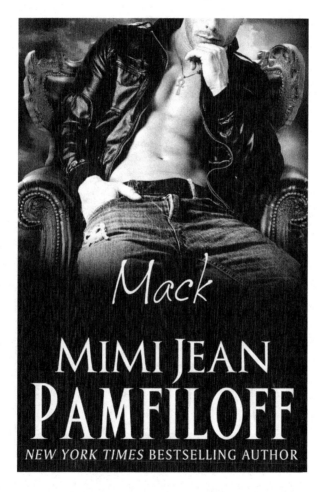

He won't break you. But his story will tear your
heart to pieces…

TOMMASO

Immortal Matchmakers, Inc. Book #2
COMING MAY 2016

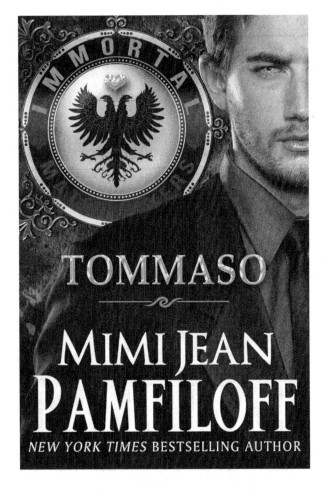

FOR BOOK EXTRAS, BUY LINKS, and NEWS:
www.mimijean.net/immortal_matchmakers.html

GOD OF WINE

Immortal Matchmakers, Inc. Book #3
COMING 2016

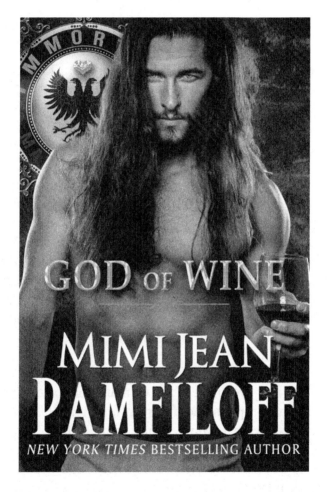

FOR BUY LINKS, BOOK EXTRAS, AND NEWS:
www.mimijean.net/immortal_matchmakers.html

ABOUT THE AUTHOR

 Mimi Jean Pamfiloff is a *New York Times* & *USA Today* best-selling author of Paranormal and Contemporary Romance. Her books have been #1 genre sellers around the world. Both traditionally and independently published, Mimi has sold over 600,000 books since publishing her first title in 2012, and she plans to spontaneously combust once she hits the one million mark. Although she obtained her international MBA and worked for over 15 years in the corporate world, she believes that it's never too late to come out of the romance closet and follow your dream.

When not screaming at her computer or hosting her very inappropriate radio show (*Man Candy Show* on Radioslot.com), Mimi spends time with her two pirates in training, her loco-for-the-chili-pepper hubby, and her rat terrier, DJ Princess Snowflake, in the San Francisco Bay Area.

She continues to hope that her books will inspire a leather pants comeback (for men) and that she might make you laugh when you need it most.

Sign up for Mimi's mailing list
for giveaways and new release news!

LEARN MORE:

mailto: mimi@mimijean.net

www.mimijean.net

twitter.com/MimiJeanRomance

http://radioslot.com/show/mancandyshow/

www.facebook.com/MimiJeanPamfiloff

CPSIA information can be obtained
at www.ICGtesting.com
Printed in the USA
FSOW03n0648140616
21513FS